HAMSTERSAURUS

SAURUS

ReX

VS.

SQUIRREL

KONG

ROL

AL

ANIMAL

ANIMAL CONTROL

BY TOM O'DONNELL

ILLUSTRATIONS BY TIM MILLER

HAMSTER-SAURUS REX >

VS.

SQUIRREL
KONG

SCHOLASTIC INC.

ISBN 978-1-338-35602-1

12 11 10 9 8 7 6 5 4 3 2   18 19 20 21 22 23

Printed in the U.S.A.   40

First Scholastic printing, October 2018

Typography by Joe Merkel

For Rudy —T.O.D.

For Andy and Detlef, my first heroes—T.M.

CONTENTS

CHAPTER 1

MR. COPELAND'S MOUTH was moving and there were definitely sounds coming out of it. If I had to guess, I'd bet those sounds were words; probably even sentences. But I wasn't listening. Instead, I was doodling in my notebook. If I *had* to give my current masterpiece a title, I'd call it *Mutant Half Hamster, Half Dinosaur Shooting Eye Lasers at Spaceship*.

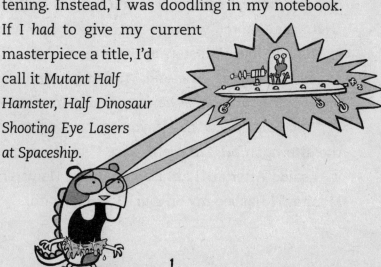

I glanced over my shoulder to the back of the room. My live model was curled up in the corner of his cage in a little furry/scaly ball—so cute/unsettling!—snoring away. I guess Mr. Copeland's voice had a similar effect on both of us. I squinted and erased Hamstersaurus Rex's mouth for the third time. I was having a lot of trouble getting the drool to look sparkly enough.

". . . And so, in conclusion: the Stamp Act," said Mr. Copeland, slamming his teacher's guide shut and startling everyone. An instant later, the final bell rang and drowsy sixth graders began to empty out into the hall.

I made my way toward Hammie's cage, but Martha Cherie, honor student and self-designated "Hamster Monitor," beat me to it.

"Smells like Hamstersaurus Rex could use a change of bedding," she said, crinkling her nose.

Hammie squinted at her, apparently insulted.

"You know, Martha, if you wanted to take the afternoon off, I'm pretty sure I could handle it," I said. "After all, I am Deputy Junior Hamster Monitor." I flashed my official ID and lanyard.

"Maybe one day, Sam," said Martha, "when you're ready." She gave me a condescending pat on the top of the head.

"Suit yourself," I said with a shrug. Then I locked eyes with Hammie Rex and gave him our secret sign. It was a simultaneous double wink that you might mistake for a blink if you didn't know what you were looking at. The little guy grunted in acknowledgment.

I turned and left.

Out in the hall, I found my best friend, Dylan D'Amato, wrestling an oversized duffel bag out of her locker.

3

"Yo, Sam," said Dylan, "you want to come up to the athletic fields and see me toss a few? We're going to be using tournament-grade discs today."

"Wish I could watch your disc golf practice, but right now I'm late to a meeting of Meeting Club," I said.

Dylan rolled her eyes as I kept walking. On the second floor, I ducked into the library and waved hello to the librarian, Mrs. Baxley. Then I made my way to 223b, a converted broom closet that held the school library's least-checked-out books. I sat down on a big stack of hardcover copies of *Collector's Guide to Paper Clips, Third Edition* to wait.

"I hereby call this meeting of Meeting Club to order," I said to no one. Yes, I was the sole member (and president, vice president, secretary, and treasurer) of Meeting Club. Contrary to what Dylan might think, the club wasn't *totally* made up. After filling out the necessary paperwork, the school had officially recognized the organization. I'd even gotten a designated meeting space and an annual thirty-five-dollar budget. Basically, Meeting Club gave me the perfect excuse for hanging around the school after hours without too much supervision.

Not long ago, getting caught alone after school would have been a very dangerous proposition for me, thanks to my longtime were-wolf-obsessed bully, Kiefer "Beefer" Vanderkoff. But Beefer was gone now. Last Science Night, he finally took things too far. SmilesCorp—makers of fine foods, swimming pool liners, laser guidance systems, and pretty much everything else you can think of—sent a representative, Roberta Fast, to our school to show off a new prototype snack: the invisible doughnut. Beefer used the occasion to try to publicly feed Hamstersaurus Rex to his pet boa constrictor, Michael Perkins. Thirty-five destroyed science projects, $4,800 worth of damage, and one broken trophy later, and Beefer Vanderkoff had been expelled from Horace Hotwater Middle School.

I checked the clock: 2:47. Martha ought to be done changing Hamstersaurus Rex's bedding and on her way to her private conversational Portuguese lesson by now. Perfect. I adjourned

Meeting Club and returned to our empty class-room. Luckily, no one had yet fixed the broken lock on the door. I ducked inside.

"Rarrrrugh," said Hammie Rex from his cage, which scientists will probably one day determine means "I love you."

"Hey, little guy. I rarrrugh you, too," I said, pulling out my Junior Deputy Hamster Monitor key and unlocking the PETCATRAZ Pro™ (reputedly the strongest small rodent cage on the market). If Martha knew I was taking Hamstersaurus Rex out for unscheduled, unauthorized purposes, her head would explode.

I opened my pocket. Hammie Rex sprang out of his cage, turned a quadruple somersault, and landed inside.

"Wow, that was one extra somersault than normal," I said. "You must be really excited to get started. Save some of that energy for the set."

I listened in the hallway. Nothing. The coast was clear, so I quietly tiptoed to my locker to grab a few things: some props, my clapboard, three bags of Funchos Marinara and Cream Cheese

Flavor-Wedges (A SmilesCorp Product™), and most important of all, my brand-new UltraLite SmartShot digital camera, the best birthday gift my mom ever got me.

Nobody was around, so I propped the back door of the school open with a rock and Hammie Rex and I headed out into the woods behind Horace Hotwater. It was a cool fall afternoon. Hammie Rex hopped out of my pocket and bounded along the ground behind me. He liked crunching through the dead leaves. We made our way through the underbrush to a clearing. It was only a few hundred feet from school, but we might as well have been in the Amazon rain forest. This was where the movie magic happened.

You see, I was currently directing my first feature film, starring none other than Hamstersaurus Rex. Not to brag, but it was definitely going to be a huge blockbuster with major crossover appeal. I quickly built the set: a cardboard diorama of a miniature cityscape. I added a few Matchbox cars and some army men to complete the scene. Then I popped the universal memory card into my camera.

"All right. Places, everyone," I said, looking around for my only actor. "Come on, time to electrify the screen with your magnetic presence, little guy."

Unfortunately, Hammie was pretty distractible in the wild. He often disappeared for long stretches to chase butterflies, stomp acorns, and sometimes gnaw on cool rocks. So I used my most effective motivational technique: I ripped open a bag of Funchos and emptied it onto the city diorama.

From out of nowhere, Hammie Rex pounced on the pile of Flavor-Wedges and started devouring them in the most gruesome manner imaginable. I set the camera low—an angle that made a five-inch hamster look like he was fifty feet tall—and hit the Record button.

"Okay. *Chinchillazilla vs. MechaChinchillazilla,* scene twenty-two, take one," I said, and I clapped my film clapper.

After finishing the Flavor-Wedges, Hamster-saurus Rex raged around the miniature city looking for more. He kicked a tiny truck out of the way. Then he stuffed a couple of army men into his mouth and roared ferociously. Great stuff! I filmed with my SmartShot in one hand and simultaneously flipped through my script with the other.

"We continue to receive reports of some sort of gigantic, mutant rodent creature thingie terrorizing our fair city of Buenos Aires!" I read in

a newscaster voice. "Will no one be able to stop Chinchillazilla and save us?"

Hamstersaurus Rex snarled and stomped a tiny sports car until its wheels popped off.

"Wait," I said, panning the camera left. "What's that on the horizon? Can it be? Another gigantic rodent monster beast? But this one seems to be made completely of . . . metal?! And cut!" I stopped recording and clapped the clapper again. I had no idea why I was clapping it but I figured it was important. Hamstersaurus Rex was still smashing the toy car into the dirt.

"Cut," I said. "Nice work, pal, but I think we might be losing a little bit of that subtlety I loved so much in your audition. The audience needs to believe that even though Chinchillazilla is a gigantic radioactive mutant, he's hurting on the inside."

Hamstersaurus Rex ignored my direction and grabbed a cardboard skyscraper in his stumpy little front paws, which he used to start pummeling the sports car. Once you got the little guy rampaging, it sure was tough to get him to stop.

"Seriously, cut," I repeated. "Hey, cut. Cut! Here,

have some food." I ripped open another bag of Flavor-Wedges and dumped them out. Hamstersaurus Rex abandoned what was left of the car went at the pile like a lunatic, crumbs and slobber flying.

"Let's move on to the scene where MechaChinchillazilla makes his first appearance," I said.

Owing to his immense acting talents (and the fact that I didn't have access to any other small rodents) Hamstersaurus Rex would also be playing the part of MechaChinchillazilla, the robotic archenemy of Chinchillazilla.

"First, we need to get you into your MechaChinchillazilla costume," I said, and I pulled a roll of aluminum foil out of my backpack.

But when I turned around, Hamstersaurus Rex was nowhere to be seen. Distracted again! I listened and heard a faint rhythmic thumping sound.

"Hamstersaurus Rex, where are you, buddy? You're needed on set," I called out. "Hammie Rex to set!"

The thumping continued. It somehow sounded like it was getting louder now.

Thump . . . thump! . . . THUMP!

"Hey, Hammie," I said, "how am I supposed to film a giant rodent monster movie without the—"

THUMP!

The ground shook beneath my feet. Deeper in the darkness of the forest, something caught my eye—a tall shape lumbering between the trees. Each heavy step it took sent vibrations through the forest floor. I couldn't make out much, but I could see that it was massive: twice as big as a full-grown adult, and covered in fur. I felt my stomach drop into my sneakers.

". . . Um. I think that's a wrap for the day, Hammie," I whispered. "We need to get out of here. Like, right now."

But there was still no sign of the little guy. I didn't know what the monster in the woods was—a Kodiak bear four thousand miles from its natural habitat, a crazed sasquatch with a taste for human flesh, or even, dare I say it, a genuine Beefer-approved real-life werewolf— but I certainly didn't want to find out. All my instincts said to run. But I just couldn't leave Hammie Rex behind.

Luckily, I still had a surefire way to summon Hamstersaurus Rex. I tore open the final bag of Funchos. A second later, the particular Flavor-Wedge smell—savory, tangy, utterly unlike anything found in nature—hit my nostrils.

"Come on, Hammie. Here, boy," I whispered, shaking the bag. "Follow your nose! But hurry!"

In the distance, the gigantic creature had stopped moving. It sniffed the air. It flicked its tail, which somehow looked too bushy to be that of a werewolf. Then it turned its massive head and looked right at me.

"Oh no," I said under my breath. "No, no, no, no."

The ground began to rumble. Thump. Thump. Thump. THUMP. THUMPTHUMPTHUMP . . .

The beast was charging right toward me, barreling through the underbrush like a runaway bulldozer. I shrieked and started to back away, but I tripped over my film clapper and fell, sprawling, onto my back. The creature burst into the clearing and let out a booming screech.

I was staring up at a twelve-foot-tall squirrel.

CHAPTER 2

"**HERE LIES SAM** Gibbs, Pulverized by a Squirrel the Size of a Small Orca." As an epitaph, it would certainly stand out in the cemetery. Still, it didn't seem like the most peaceful way to go.

A foot from my head, the colossal rodent flattened all of cardboard Buenos Aires with a single stomp, sending shock waves through the ground. I was frozen with terror, speechless and unable to move. I could only assume my skull would get stomped next, which was too bad. I really liked my skull.

Just then, I heard a snarl. An orange blur shot

through the air and landed on the ground between me and the giant squirrel. It was Hamstersaurus Rex! His fangs were bared and the fur on his haunches was bristling. The little guy meant to battle the beast.

The giant squirrel paused and blinked. It seemed genuinely confused by this aggressive display. Honestly, I was, too. What was Hammie Rex thinking? Dino-strength or no, he was approximately 1/4,000th of the monster's size. The squirrel casually raised its other foot to squash the little guy like a bug. Hamstersaurus Rex roared in defiance and didn't budge. I had to do something.

I tossed the bag of Funchos and snatched Hammie out of the way, right before the squirrel's foot came down like a pile driver. THWAM!

In an instant, I was on my feet, racing back toward the school at top speed. Branches whipped at my face and brambles tore at my clothes as I ran. Hammie growled and squirmed against my grip, still spoiling for a fight.

I reached the school only to find that it was shut and locked. The rock I had used to prop it open had been kicked out of the way. The janitor, Mr. Grogan, must have done it. I pounded on the door but no one came. From the woods behind me, I heard the bloodcurdling cry of the giant squirrel again. I stuffed Hammie into my shirt pocket and took off once more.

I ran all the way around the school—looking over my shoulder the whole way—and I didn't stop until I got to the athletic fields. My lungs were burning and I was soaked with sweat by the time I found Dylan. She was tossing discs at a basket-shaped target a few dozen feet away. Across the field, Tina Gomez and Dwight Feinberg, the other two members of the newly formed disc golf team, were working on their fundamentals.

"So, you just couldn't hold back your Disc-whipper spirit," said Dylan, grinning as she saw me approach. She threw her disc at a sharp angle at the ground. It bounced off the turf and took flight, dinging the target and landing in the basket. "By the way, we're called the Horace Hotwater Discwhippers now. Pretty great team name, huh? I came up with it."

"Big . . . ," I wheezed, struggling to catch my breath.

"*Big?* Sam, we're gonna be huge! Coach Weekes and I even found another school that has a team and luckily they're only three states away. In two weeks, the Discwhippers are going to face off against the West Blunkton Flingmasters in an exhibition tournament right here in town. SmilesCorp has agreed to sponsor it. We're gonna have uniforms and everything!"

". . . squirrel!" I managed to get out between gasps.

"Oh, okay. Um, naked mole rat, I guess," said Dylan. "Your turn?"

I doubled over and put my hands on my knees.

"Look, 'Name a Rodent' is a fine game, Sam," said Dylan, "but I've kind of got to get back to practice."

NAME A RODENT

BEAVER   MOUSE

"I was attacked by some sort of . . . twelve-foot-tall . . . Squirrel . . . Kong!" I sputtered.

Dylan cocked her head. "Well, that's exciting!"

"No, it was terrifying!" I said.

"D'Amato! Are we here to practice our forehand throws or our jaw muscles?" Coach Weekes was stalking across the field toward us.

Dylan scowled. "Sorry, Coach."

"Gibbs, you're not a Discwhipper," said Weekes. "What the heck are you doing here?"

"A giant squirrel attacked me," I said.

"I'm assuming that's a metaphor for something. Just remember: when we face adversity, adversity also faces us. Now get your chakras off my field!" He bowed and pointed to the bleachers.

NAKED MOLE RAT

PORCUPINE

"Chakras?" I said.

"Coach recently found his spiritual side," said Dylan under her breath. "Don't worry, Sam. We'll talk later."

Still shaking from the adrenaline, I took a seat. I spent the last twenty minutes of disc golf practice jumping at every noise and scanning my surroundings for any sign of the monster. On the field, Coach Weekes was getting increasingly frustrated with the two non-Dylan team members, peppering his usual bluster with a few strange New Age-y phrases. Inside my pocket, Hammie Rex was still in a fighting mood, snuffling and growling.

"Look, you don't have to prove anything to me," I whispered to him. "I *know* you're tough. But a squirrel that big? One stomp from that thing and you're a fuzzy pancake."

A clanging noise came from the field. Dwight had somehow lodged one of his discs in the scoreboard. Coach Weekes sighed.

"All right, that's it for today. Get out of my sight," said Weekes, shaking his head. "I want you all to go home and meditate on not being terrible at disc golf. Namaste."

The other two Discwhippers shuffled off the field. Dylan jogged over and sat down on the bleachers beside me. I was finally able to relay the whole Squirrel Kong attack to her.

"Really?" said Dylan, stroking her chin. "*Chinchillazilla vs. MechaChinchillazilla?* That's the title you want to go with for your movie? It's a little clunky."

"What? Dylan, focus on the rampaging Squirrel Kong that tried to crush me, not what I decided to call my . . ." I trailed off as I had a sudden, unpleasant realization.

"What is it?" said Dylan.

"My UltraLite SmartShot digital camera," I said with a sigh. "I must have left it down there in the woods. I guess I dropped it in all the commotion. Now I won't be able to finish my feature film debut."

"Sure you will," said Dylan, grinning.

"How?" I asked.

"We're going to go back and get it." She stood and cracked her knuckles.

"Again, maybe you weren't listening to me when I told you about the heinous giant squirrel that haunts the woods behind our school looking for sixth graders to flatten," I said.

"Oh, please, I'm not scared of some big squirrel," said Dylan. "And neither is he!"

She pointed to my pocket. Hammie Rex's head was poking out. His eyes were narrowed with resolve and his fuzzy little lips were pulled back to reveal a row of pointy dinosaur teeth. He burped an angry burp. The little guy was definitely looking for a rematch.

CHAPTER 3

"LOOK, IF I don't make it out of these woods," I whispered, "you can have all my drawings. An artist's work usually goes up in value after they . . . you know."

"Calm down, Sam," said Dylan. "I'll tell you what I told you back in preschool when you got that sand pail stuck on your head: you're not going to die."

"That pail was very small! I could have easily run out of oxygen in there!"

"Look, my dad is going to be here in, like, five minutes to pick me up from disc golf practice, so can we just grab your camera and go?"

I swallowed and stepped into the tall weeds.

Dylan followed. As we made our way toward the clearing, each cracking branch sounded like the approach of a monster. Every few feet, I stopped to listen for the telltale thump of the beast's heavy footsteps. Hamstersaurus Rex scanned the woods from my pocket, ready for action.

"No fighting," I whispered to Hamstersaurus Rex. "Remember?"

He snorted. After what seemed like forever, the three of us made it to the clearing. It was empty. Dylan stared at me and shrugged.

"Well, looks like these woods are giant squirrel–free," she said. "Probably heard I was coming and got scared."

"Squirrel Kong was just here," I said, "I swear."

Just then Hammie Rex grunted. Dylan and I looked at each other, our eyes wide. His ears were twitching. The little guy heard something. Pretty soon we both heard it, too. It was a faint buzzing sound coming from overhead. Both of us looked up. A small remote-controlled quadcopter zipped by, sixty feet above us, and then disappeared from view.

"Hmm. Maybe *that's* what you saw," offered Dylan.

"Did that look *anything* like a giant squirrel to you?" I said, exasperated.

"If you squint and turn your head sideways, it sort of looks like a *flying* squirrel—"

"Squirrel Kong is real!" I cried. The sound of my voice echoed through the woods, startling me.

"Okay, okay. Chill out, Sam," said Dylan. "Look, the good news is, we found your digital camera." She reached down and pulled my UltraLite SmartShot out of a bush and handed it to me.

"Thanks," I said, dusting a few leaves off it. "If this thing is broken, my mom is going to make Squirrel Kong look like a pushover."

I held my breath and turned it on. It seemed to be functional, but it was displaying an error message on the screen. "Hang on. The memory card is missing. Do you see it anywhere?"

"Nope," said Dylan, scanning the bush where she'd found the camera. "Doesn't look like it's here."

"It must have fallen out," I said. "That stinks."

"What? Memory cards aren't expensive, are they?" said Dylan.

"No, it's just . . . that card had my entire movie on it."

"Sorry, Sam. But if you have to start over, at least you'll have the chance to think of a better title. What if you called your movie *Fatal Payback: The Revenge?*"

"That, uh, kind of sounds like a different direction," I said.

"Look, we've seen the giant-monsters-battling-each-other thing before. I'm thinking now that Hammie Rex is a renegade cop who has been pushed too far. Maybe he has a tough-as-nails human female partner, Vanessa McSteel."

"Played by you, I'm guessing?"

"Whoa. That's a very interesting idea," said Dylan, stroking her chin. "I hadn't even thought of that."

I sighed. By now, all the other disc golfers had gone home and the school was locked. There would be no getting Hammie Rex back in his cage for the night. I'd have to bring him home with me.

So I caught a ride with Dylan and her dad.

When I got to my house I made a beeline for our garage. My mom was still allergic to all pets except our ancient hairless cat, Raisin. So when I brought Hammie Rex home on a secret unauthorized overnight, I used a special hypoallergenic hamster habitat I'd created. Basically, I'd hidden a hamster cage inside an old cardboard box marked "Extension Cords." I'd poked several holes in the box and lined it with air filters to catch as much of Hammie's stray dander as possible. I'd even put a few rubber dinosaurs in there, too, so the little guy would feel at home. I took Hamstersaurus Rex out of my pocket and placed him in the box.

"Thanks for saving me today," I said, scratching him behind his little ear. "But you have to forget about Squirrel Kong, okay?"

Hammie snarled at the name.

"Seriously, Hammie. Besides, we're never going to see that awful creature again, so it doesn't even matter."

His growl sounded doubtful. I closed the lid.

"Hiya, Bunnybutt," said my mom as I walked in the door. "How was your Meeting Club?"

"Pretty good. Everyone in the club is super cool but very down to earth. It's a very chill vibe," I said.

"Chill vibe! Great! Anything else happen at school today?"

"Well, a twelve-foot-tall squirrel tried to squish me," I said.

"That's crazy," said my mom, now staring at me with grave concern. "Because the *same exact thing* happened to me!" She burst out laughing and didn't stop for the next ten minutes. My mom's got a weird sense of humor.

I slept fitfully that night, racked with

nightmares about giant rodents. The next morning, I caught the bus to school. Hamster-saurus Rex—hidden in my shirt pocket—dozed peacefully, seemingly untroubled by any bad dreams of his own.

Omar Powell did a double take as he took the seat in front of me. "Yikes, Sam," he said. "You look terrible."

"I guess I didn't sleep well," I said with a shrug.

"Something on your mind?"

"A giant squirrel tried to kill me," I said.

"Huh. Sounds stressful," said Omar as he pulled out his Gamehouser Mega IV and started to play that game where you fling penguins at works of fine art.

Omar didn't believe me. My mom didn't believe me. And I could tell that even though she said she believed me, Dylan had her doubts. The worst part was that I was starting to wonder if maybe they were right.

People often told me that I had an "overactive imagination" because I liked to draw and make dioramas and sure, maybe because I bent the truth a little here and there. Maybe those people were right. Maybe it wasn't a giant squirrel I saw? Maybe it was just a really . . . big . . . dog? Or maybe it was two adult men in a squirrel costume . . . rehearsing for a play?

No. I *had* seen a giant squirrel! And Hammie Rex had seen it, too. I sighed. It probably didn't even matter at this point. What were the odds that I'd ever see Squirrel Kong again, anyway? I wasn't planning on hanging out in the woods behind school anytime soon. I took a deep breath and tried to put the whole thing out of my mind and think of whatever the opposite of a giant squirrel is. (A very tiny rhinoceros?)

But I couldn't concentrate. There was a commotion at the front of the bus that caused Hammie Rex to start awake in my pocket. He peeped out from under the flap. Now kids were crowding toward the windows and pointing as the bus pulled into the school parking lot. We

rolled past two parked police cars with their lights flashing.

"Wow. Look at that!" said Drew McCoy.

A massive hole had been smashed through the wall of Horace Hotwater Middle School. It was approximately the size and shape of Squirrel Kong.

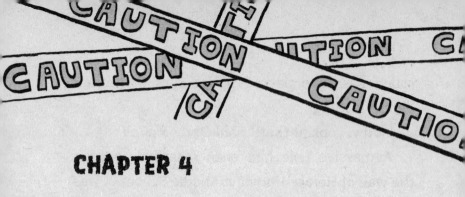

CHAPTER 4

INSIDE THE SCHOOL, yellow hazard tape blocked access to Room 117, the science lab. A dozen kids pushed in close to get a better look, but Mr. Grogan stood in front of the door, blocking their view.

"Move along, kiddies. Nothing to see," said Mr. Grogan as he added another layer of tape. "Room 117 is off-limits until further notice. Principal's orders."

I craned my neck as I walked past and managed to catch a glimpse inside. Not only had something big burst right through the wall, whatever it was had utterly destroyed the place! Tables and equipment were overturned and smashed. Books and papers and broken glass were strewn everywhere. It looked like a war zone.

While the other kids were still jockeying for a peek at the wrecked lab, I made a quick detour to our classroom. As usual, it was empty. I was early, and Mr. Copeland never arrived at school before 7:50. I ducked inside and quickly put Hammie back into his PETCATRAZ Pro™ and locked the cage door.

At the lockers, the rest of sixth grade was abuzz with theories about the incident.

"I heard it was a gas leak," said Julie Bailey, pantomiming. "Kaboomers!"

"No way," said Jimmy Choi. "My cousin Todd is a policeman and he told me it was a freak mini-tornado that did it."

"It *had* to be an earthquake," said Caroline Moody. "This whole school is completely structurally unsound. Maple Bluffs sits on a major fault line, you know. Another little tremor and the building is going to collapse!" She put her notebook over her head for protection.

"Guys, think logically," said Jared Kopernik. "It was ghosts."

"Sam, how do you think the lab got destroyed?" asked Tina Gomez as I stuffed my backpack into my locker.

"Giant squirrel attack," I offered.

The other kids burst out laughing, just like my mom. I sighed.

"That's it!"

We all turned to see Ms. Becker, the sixth-grade science teacher, down the hall. She was yelling at Principal Truitt.

"First, invisible snakes at Science Night and now *this?*" cried Ms. Becker. "My whole classroom has been ruined. If I'd been here, I could have been killed. This school is completely insane. Nobody's safe!"

"Calm down," muttered Principal Truitt, taking her by the elbow. "We should discuss this *privately* in my office so we don't scare any of the—"

"There's nothing to discuss. I'm telling you right that now that I quit! Things like this don't happen at L. L. Dupree Middle School, you know."

"Please, Maria," said Principal Truitt. "Be reasonable. We don't know what happened."

"Of course we do! It was obviously that weird hamster from Arnold's classroom that did it!" said Ms. Becker. "We all know how freakishly strong the little vermin is. Everyone says it whipped a fifty-pound boa constrictor around by its tail like a spaghetti noodle. As long as that *beast* is at Horace Hotwater, I won't be!" With that she stormed off down the hall.

Weird hamster? Vermin? Beast? She couldn't possibly mean Hamstersaurus Rex, could she? I was shocked. Sure, the little guy was dino-strong—strong enough to do a few knuckle-ups for me, maybe knock a wooden door off its hinges once in a while. But there was no way he could smash through a brick wall! Plus, why would he even want to? He was a hamster of peace (mostly)!

"Whoa, Ms. Becker just quit, you guys," said

Dylan, joining the rest of us at the lockers. "I wonder if science class is permanently canceled."

"Makes sense," said Jimmy, nodding solemnly. "I bet it *was* Hamstersaurus Rex."

"You know, I never liked Hamstersaurus Rex," said Tina.

"Yeah," said Caroline Moody, dropping her voice low. "He's always had *anger issues*."

"He has not!" I cried. "It wasn't Hamstersaurus Rex that did this and I know it!"

"Guys, listen to Sam," said Dylan. "He was with—"

I shushed Dylan as I saw Martha Cherie approaching. She looked pale and shell-shocked.

"Sam, may I have a word?" said Martha quietly, her jaw clenched.

"Um. Okay, sure."

Martha took me aside and whispered, "I'm really worried, Sam. I think I might have left the PETCATRAZ Pro™ unlocked yesterday when I changed Hamstersaurus Rex's bedding."

"No, Martha. Trust me, you didn't," I said. "You would have never forgotten a thing like that.

Hammie Rex is locked in his cage. You can go check right now."

"I just talked to Mr. Grogan. He noticed that the cage was empty while he was cleaning our classroom yesterday evening. He didn't see Hamstersaurus Rex anywhere," said Martha. She sounded more upset than I'd ever heard her. "You and I both know that the PETCATRAZ Pro™ is rated the strongest small rodent cage on the market. If Hamstersaurus Rex was out, that means the cage was unlocked."

"Yeah, okay, maybe he was out of his cage, but that's only because . . ." I trailed off. Unfortunately, my explanation involved admitting that Hammie was with me all night, and that I was totally abusing my Junior Deputy Hamster Monitor privileges by taking the little guy home when I wasn't supposed to. Who knew what the penalty for abducting a class pet was?

"Listen to me," I said. "I just *know* Hamstersaurus Rex didn't wreck the lab, okay?"

"How?" asked Martha Cherie. "How do you know?" Her voice cracked like she was about to cry.

"Uh, I mean, because he's a . . . solid dude," I said. It sounded pretty weak, even to me. She didn't seem convinced.

"This feels weird," said Martha.

"What feels weird?"

"Making a mistake," she said. "I've never made a mistake before, Sam. Is this how the rest of you feel all the time?"

Before I could answer the first bell rang.

As we took our seats, I noticed all the other kids eyeing Hammie Rex with suspicion. They muttered under their breath and shook their heads and pointed. Was he already guilty in their minds? In his cage, the little guy looked agitated and confused. He could sense something was wrong.

"Okay, kids," said Mr. Copeland, frowning. "I know how excited you all are to learn more about pronouns, but there's something serious we need to discuss first."

"Snails?" said Wilbur Weber.

"No, Wilbur. Not snails," said Mr. Copeland. "As you probably all noticed, there's a giant hole in the side of the school. The science lab has been completely destroyed. We don't yet know who, or what, caused this damage. But unfortunately, some people think the culprit may have been our class pet, Hamstersaurus Rex."

"Mr. Copeland, he's innocent!" I cried.

"Sam, we all know how much you love the hamster. Hey, I'll admit it, I'm fond of the little guy myself," said Mr. Copeland. "But we need to wait until we have more information about what happened before we draw any conclusions. Now, does anyone have any concerns they'd like to share?"

"Mr. Copeland," said Tina Gomez in a stage whisper. "I feel like Hamstersaurus Rex is looking at me right now and he looks angry. I'm literally paralyzed with fear!"

"He's not angry," I said. "He's hungry. If he ever acts nuts, it's just because he's hungry."

"So he wants to *eat* me?" said Tina.

The other kids gasped.

"Look, Tina, the cage is made of an unbreakable titanium alloy," said Mr. Copeland. "I checked their website. As long as it's locked you're perfectly safe."

Just then, an anguished yelp rang out across the classroom. Everyone turned toward the sound. It had come from Martha Cherie.

". . . Um, is everything okay, Martha?" said Mr. Copeland.

"No, Mr. Copeland, everything is not okay," said Martha. "May I please address the class?"

"Okay, fine," said Mr. Copeland. "What's on your mind?"

Martha stood up and cleared her throat. Her voice trembled as she spoke. "Classmates, I once swore a sacred oath: an oath to protect and serve our class hamster. But the oath is more than that. It also extends to you, the students and faculty of Horace Hotwater Middle School. I am sad to report that yesterday I failed in my duty as Hamster Monitor. I left the cage unlocked and thus I failed to protect you from Hamstersaurus Rex. It is with great sorrow that I hereby tender my resignation as Hamster Monitor." Martha ceremoniously removed her

Hamster Monitor ID lanyard and placed it on Mr. Copeland's desk.

"Um, you made this lanyard yourself, Martha," said Mr. Copeland. "You really don't have to give it back to me."

"Please don't try to talk me out of it, Arnold," said Martha. "As painful as this is, it's for the best."

"Martha, you can't resign," I said, surprising myself a little. "Hammie Rex needs people to look out for him."

"You're right, Sam," said Martha, nodding. "As my last official action as Hamster Monitor, I hereby promote you, Sam Gibbs, from the rank of Junior Deputy Hamster Monitor to the rank of Hamster Monitor, First Class."

"What?" I said.

"Is Hamster Monitor a real thing?" whispered Omar. Julie Bailey shrugged.

"May you do a better job than I did," said Martha, blinking back tears as she shook my hand.

"Martha, please," I said. "You can't do this. I—"

"Sorry to interrupt," said Principal Truitt.

The whole class turned to see her standing in the doorway with Mr. Grogan by her side. He was wearing a baseball catcher's mask and pads with two thick oven mitts on his hands.

"Not a problem, Principal," said Mr. Copeland. "What's up?"

"Unfortunately," said Principal Truitt, "I'm going to need to take your class hamster away for . . . evaluation."

Mr. Grogan cautiously crept toward the cage. He was acting like it held a cobra or a great white shark instead of a hamster. Hamstersaurus Rex growled again, confused and upset. Mr. Grogan jumped back in terror.

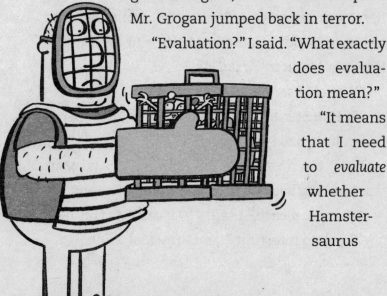

"Evaluation?" I said. "What exactly does evaluation mean?"

"It means that I need to *evaluate* whether Hamstersaurus

Rex poses a threat to the students of this school, Mr. Gibbs," said Principal Truitt. "And if he does, then he no longer has a place at Horace Hotwater."

Inside his cage, Hammie whined pitifully and pressed his face against the bars. Mr. Grogan hefted the PETCATRAZ Pro™ and disappeared down the hallway.

"Forgive the interruption. Please, carry on," said Principal Truitt as she closed the door behind her.

Now it was me who tried not to cry.

CHAPTER 5

IT **WAS A** bleak day. Whenever there was a
moment between classes, I tried to talk to Martha about Hamstersaurus Rex. Each time, she
changed the subject or avoided me. At lunch I
managed to corner her and bring it up again.

"No, Sam. I currently have no plans to un-resign
as Hamster Monitor," she said with a strained grin.
"I'm honestly looking forward to spending more
time with my other extracurricular activities.
On top of my current load, I'm taking up debate
and modern dance and competitive origami, and
I just landed a very prestigious internship at the
Antique Doll Museum."

"But Hammie didn't do it! He didn't wreck the lab. It was a giant mutant squirrel beast called Squirrel Kong," I said. "Well, I call it Squirrel Kong. I don't know what name is on its birth certificate or whatever."

"Squirrels don't have birth certificates," said Martha, capping her hands over her ears. "And this all sounds like official Hamster Monitor business that a

mere civilian like me doesn't need to know about." With that, she disappeared to go sit alone at an empty table.

I sighed. Dylan put her tray down on the table beside me.

"Sorry, Sam," said Dylan. "Man, did you ever think that you'd actually *want* Martha Cherie to keep on Hamster Monitoring?"

"No," I said. "But these days Hammie needs all the help he can get. The other kids are acting like he's an ax murderer or something."

"Well, you know I've always got the little guy's back," said Dylan. "We'll figure out what happened to the science lab and clear his good name."

"What do you mean *figure it out?*" I snapped. "We already know it was Squirrel Kong!"

"Right. Exactly," said Dylan, taken aback. "That's what I meant."

The rest of the day passed in much the same way. I took a basketball to the face in gym class, I apparently forgot to do the geometry homework, and I accidentally sat in taffy. My mom made cauliflower and beets for dinner, which didn't improve things much. All I could think about was Hammie Rex, alone and afraid, getting "evaluated." That night I dreamed about more monster squirrels.

When I woke up the next day, I knew what I had to do. As soon

as I got to school I headed straight to the principal's office. In the waiting area, I sat across from a strange man with a ponytail who was wearing sunglasses indoors. When he saw me staring, he gave me a double thumbs-up. Weird.

"Sam, the principal will see you now," said Truitt's secretary.

Principal Truitt's office was cold and spare. On a shelf behind her imposing wooden desk I saw the PETCATRAZ Pro™. Inside it, Hammie Rex looked pitiful and deflated. She probably wasn't feeding him enough. The little guy needed at least eight square meals a day to stay chipper. Hammie Rex perked up as he saw me enter the room. I gave him a quick double wink.

"Good morning, Mr. Gibbs," said Principal Truitt. "I must say, not many students send themselves to the principal's office. To what do I owe the pleasure?"

I took a deep breath. "Principal Truitt, I have a confession to make."

"Aha! So it's you who's been stealing all the mustard packets from the cafeteria?" said

Principal Truitt, leaping to her feet.

"What? No," I said. "It's about Hamstersaurus Rex."

"Oh," said Principal Truitt. She sat back down.

"You see, there's a reason he wasn't in his cage the other night when the science lab got wrecked."

"Go on," said Principal Truitt.

"It's because I took him home with me. I know I'm not supposed to do that, but I did. Hamstersaurus Rex couldn't have wrecked the lab because he was with me all night. So give me detention or suspend me or whatever, but *please* don't blame Hamstersaurus Rex for what happened."

Principal Truitt nodded. "I think I see what's going on here, Mr. Gibbs."

"You do?"

She nodded. "You love this hamster so much that you think you can make up an alibi for him. It's very common for students to try to protect their friends when they get into trouble. I've seen it a hundred times before."

"But I'm not making anything up!" I cried. "A mysterious mega-squirrel who secretly lives in the woods behind the school wrecked the lab!"

Principal Truitt squinted at me. "Sam, please. No more lies," she said. She swiveled in her chair and squinted at the little guy. "Over the last twenty-four hours, my observations of Hamstersaurus Rex have confirmed my worst fears. I have found this creature to be impulsive, aggressive, and alarmingly strong."

"I know," I said. "That's what makes him so cool."

"Around the presence of food, especially, he loses all control," she said.

Principal Truitt slid open her left desk drawer. I saw that it was filled with bags of Funchos Spicy Wasabi and French Onion Flavor-Wedges. She grabbed a bag and held it up.

"Observe," she said as she ripped it open. Sure enough, Hammie Rex snarled and started kicking the bars of his cage, drool oozing from his mouth.

Principal Truitt deliberately folded the bag closed and replaced it in the drawer.

"Okay, yes, impulse control is something he needs to work on. He doesn't get that Flavor-Wedges are a 'sometimes food.'"

"Regardless," said Principal Truitt. "I've come to the conclusion that Hamstersaurus Rex poses a significant danger to our school. And I'm not merely basing it on his junk food aggression, nor the rampant destruction I witnessed at Science Night."

"That wasn't his fault! Beefer tried to feed him to his dumb snake."

"New evidence has come to light, Mr. Gibbs, that makes me certain that Hamstersaurus Rex is guilty of destroying the lab."

"New evidence? What new evidence?"

Principal Truitt took a deep breath. "Sam, I'm warning you: the footage you're about to see is disturbing. It shows a very dark and twisted side of Hamstersaurus Rex's character. You may never think of him as your cuddly little friend again."

She dimmed the lights and turned the screen of her laptop to face me. A shaky digital video started to play. Sure enough, it was footage of Hamstersaurus Rex, but from the angle it was shot, he looked huge and intimidating. Monstrous, even. He snarled and stomped around with a psychotic glint in his eye. Suddenly, he picked up a station wagon and hurled it the ground, causing it to burst into a cloud of metal shrapnel. Then he smashed right through three buildings to find a group of

soldiers cowering behind their army jeep. With an evil snarl, he bit the head off their commander (the one with binoculars) while his men looked on in mute horror. I was watching *Chinchillazilla vs. MechaChinchillazilla*.

"Sickening," said Principal Truitt under her breath.

"It's not sickening, it's just a movie I made!" I said.

"Enough, Mr. Gibbs. You can't protect Hamstersaurus Rex anymore."

Onscreen, Hammie Rex was kicking down a cardboard building marked "Laboratory." I'll admit, it didn't look good.

"See?" said Principal Truitt. "He clearly hates science."

"But he's *acting*!" I said. "That's the lab where MechaChinchillazilla was—look, I can show you the script—I mean, the script has changed a lot since we shot this, so this scene's not in there anymore, but still—this must have come from a digital memory card that somebody found, right?"

Principal Truitt paused. "Mr. Grogan did find a memory card in the woods behind the school, but that's not the point. The point is that if Hamstersaurus Rex is capable of this . . . then he's obviously capable of destroying our lab, too. I worry what else he's capable of."

"Come on! He's not *capable* of anything weird except walking on his back legs and occasionally eating his body weight in Funchos and—"

"Enough, Mr. Gibbs!" said Principal Truitt.

From his cage, Hammie Rex let out an ear-splitting roar. Principal Truitt spun in her seat, terrified. The little guy was baring his pointed teeth at her. His tail was whipping back and forth. He could sense that I was upset and he wanted to help me. Unfortunately, it was the worst possible time for an outburst.

"Easy, Hammie," I said in a soothing tone. "It's okay, boy. Calm down."

"This is exactly what terrifies me, Mr. Gibbs," said Principal Truitt as she smoothed her jacket and regained her composure. Then she reached into her desk drawer and pulled out a glossy

brochure. On it was a picture of an ominous-looking farmhouse surrounded by a barbed-wire fence.

"I'm sorry. I've made up my mind," she said.

"There's a special center in Indiana. It's called the Irma Bergstrom Memorial Home for Troubled Small Pets. Their highly trained staff can provide proper care for hamsters who have shown violent or dangerous behavior. I called them and luckily they have a spot opening up soon."

"What are you talking about?"

"They're willing to take Hamstersaurus Rex. At the Home he can be safely isolated so he doesn't hurt anyone ever again."

"What do you mean *again*? He didn't hurt anyone in the first place!" I cried. "He's innocent! You can't just send him away!"

"I can and I will. Mr. Gibbs, I refuse to put the

students of this school in jeopardy, regardless of your misplaced affection for an unruly class pet. Our insurance doesn't cover rogue hamster attacks! What if there had been someone inside that lab when Hamstersaurus Rex destroyed it?"

Hamstersaurus Rex snarled again.

"What if there weren't titanium bars between that hamster and me right now?" said Principal Truitt.

The first bell rang.

"It's time for you to go to class, Mr. Gibbs. In time I think you'll see the wisdom of my decision."

I stood and walked toward the door, so upset I could barely think. I paused.

"When are you sending him to that hamster jail?" I asked.

Principal Truitt frowned. "In seven days."

I nodded and left. So that was that: I had one week to prove that Squirrel Kong was real and save Hamstersaurus Rex.

CHAPTER 6

"SAM, LOOK," WHISPERED Dylan, pointing to a dark shape in the woods behind Horace Hotwater. "Is that Squirrel Kong?"

I squinted. "No, that's a tree."

We'd already spent two weekday afternoons and most of Saturday and Sunday searching the area. So far, we hadn't seen any squirrels that were even slightly above average size.

"Hmm. Okay," said Dylan, "is *that* Squirrel Kong?"

"Nope. That's a different tree."

"Okay . . . is that Squirrel Kong?"

"No," I said. "That's the first tree you asked about!"

Dylan frowned.

"Sorry," I said. "Thanks for doing this with me. I know it's boring to search the same woods every day and I really appreciate your help. I'm just frustrated. Seriously, where does a twelve-foot-tall squirrel hide?"

I checked my UltraLite SmartShot for the hundredth time. The new memory card was in place, ready to capture hard video evidence if Squirrel Kong ever made another appearance. Dylan glanced at her watch.

"Sam, I've really got to take off. Practice is starting in five minutes. The Discwhippers have got a ton of work to do before the exhibition tournament. Dwight's high-release backhand isn't where it needs to be, and honestly I'm a little worried Coach Weekes doesn't actually know how the scoring works."

"Actually, I've been meaning to talk to you about Coach Weekes," I said. "Something has been puzzling me about that guy."

"Oh. His new earring is called an 'ankh.' It's the ancient Egyptian symbol for life."

"Not that. It's about Squirrel Kong."

"Go on."

"So a twelve-foot-tall squirrel obviously must be some kind of mutation, right?"

"I guess."

"And the only other mutant rodent I know got mutated when he ate something from Coach Weekes's office. It was a SmilesCorp product, some kind of weight-lifting powder called Dinoblast Powerpacker."

"Sure, I remember. 'It gives you prehistoric strength,' right?"

"Yep. Hammie gobbled that junk and it made him go all half-dinosaur. What if another one of Weekes's weird dietary supplements is what created Squirrel Kong? Like maybe a normal squirrel ate something and then grew to the size of two refrigerators."

"So you want to poke around his office and try to find out?" said Dylan. "I don't know, Sam. I'm not sure Coach Weekes is even into all those powders and shakes anymore. Don't get me wrong, he's still really, *really* weird. Just not in quite the same way. After he confessed to cheating at the '83 Little Mister Muscles, he's gotten way more . . . organic."

"It's just a hunch," I said. "But I've got only one day left before Principal Truitt sends Hammie away for good. I wouldn't ask if it wasn't important."

"What do you have in mind?"

"Tomorrow, during gym class, how about a little distraction?"

Dylan grinned. "You got it," she said. "In fact, you can consider it my audition to be in your next movie."

"Awesome! You're the best," I said. "Seriously, Hammie Rex and I owe you big-time. Whatever you want, just name—"

"I need you to get to the disc golf exhibition tournament early," she said. "We just found out that SmilesCorp is sending somebody super important to the event, their CEO, Nils Winroth. Those stands need to be full for his opening remarks."

"I'll be there, cheering your name," I said.

"Also, I need you to paint your face in Disc-whipper colors: maroon and mauve."

"Uh. Okay, fine. Those are both kind of purple right?"

"No way!" said Dylan. "Purple is the West Blunkton Flingmasters color. Do *not* wear purple face paint!"

"Okay, okay, I get it," I said, even though I didn't.

Dylan gave me a nod and then trudged off toward the athletic fields.

I kept on searching for Squirrel Kong until it was nearly dark. I found nothing. That night I combed the internet (yet again) for any reputable news stories about giant squirrels in Maple Bluffs or the surrounding areas. Nothing. As always, the only result that turned up was on a crackpot message board called truthblasters.com. Someone claimed to have seen a "mysterious creature" stalking through the weeds behind their house and somehow this proved that the moon landing was faked and the president was actually a super-intelligent dolphin. Even if true, it wasn't very helpful.

True to her word, in gym class the next day Dylan faked a spectacular knee injury during badminton.

"Oweeeeee!" Dylan screamed, rolling around on the floor and dramatically clutching her leg. "I took a birdie to the patella!"

Coach Weekes emitted a high-pitched shriek and rushed to Dylan's side. "D'Amato? What's wrong?" He turned to Drew McCoy, her unlucky badminton opponent. "What did you do to her, *you monster?*"

"I dunno," mumbled Drew. "Didn't even look like it hit her—"

"Oweeeeeee!" wailed Dylan. "Big ouches!"

"D'Amato?" said Coach Weekes, clutching Dylan's hand as the rest of the class crowded around. "D'Amato, can you hear me?"

". . . Mom? Is that you?" said Dylan. "Mommy, am I ever going to play disc golf again?"

"Don't you worry about that, D'Amato," said Coach Weekes, his voice cracking. "You're going to come back from this, kid. You're going to be better than ever. Your chi is strong. You hear me? *Your chi is strong!*"

"I feel cold," whispered Dylan, now staring blankly at the ceiling. "So . . . cold."

"Doctor!" cried Coach Weekes. "We need a doctor! Is anyone here a doctor?"

The rest of the class looked at one another, confused.

"Um, Coach," said Julie Bailey, "we're all twelve years old."

"You know what?" I said. "It looks to me like Dylan might need some bandages."

"Actually," said Martha, "there aren't any cuts or bruises, so—"

"Bandages!" I said, cutting Martha off. "Coach, you got any bandages in your office?"

Coach Weekes squinted at me. "Smart thinking, Gibbs," he said. "Don't just stand there, go and get me those bandages! Bottom right desk drawer! Don't touch any of my mandalas!"

I had maybe a minute, maybe two tops. I dashed to Coach Weekes's office and closed the door behind me. I was shocked at what I saw inside.

Weekes had completely redecorated the place. Gone were the dusty old trophies and 1980s weight-lifting posters. Now the room was filled with geodes and woven blankets and dream catchers. Instead of Weekes's rusty dumbbells that had sat in the corner as long as I could remember, there was a yoga mat and a set of bongos. Weirdest of all, his office no longer smelled like weight gainer and

feet. Now it smelled kind of like incense and feet.

I scoured the shelves looking for any strange dietary supplements that could potentially mutate a squirrel. They were all gone. Weekes had replaced them with books (books?!) that had titles like *Achieving Your Mental Soulpath* and *Who Really Built the Alamo? (It Was Aliens.)*

Weekes's desk was equally empty of any powders, pills, or potions that might create a Squirrel Kong. Instead, I found a crystal pendant and a day planner that only had one entry. On the Thursday after next, Coach Weekes had written in "3 p.m.—Achieve Total Consciousness." I was about to leave when I found an MP3 player in the bottom drawer. On impulse, I put the earbuds in and pushed Play.

I heard the soothing sound of the ocean and instantly felt more relaxed.

"You are a rock in the middle of the sea," a calm, steady voice said. "Be the rock."

It was some kind of strange meditation tape.

"You have total control of your impulses . . . A rock doesn't bite its toenails . . . You are a rock . . ."

I listened for a few more minutes before yanking the earbuds out. There was no evidence in Coach Weekes's office. Whatever Squirrel Kong's origin, it didn't involve Weekes's questionable dietary supplements. The man really had turned over a New Age leaf. Also he bit his toenails. Blech. I grabbed the roll of bandages and headed back out to the gym.

Frustrated, I watched the hours of the day dwindle. Martha refused to talk about the case. (She was pretty talkative about her Antique Doll Museum internship, however.) Everyone else frowned and shook their heads when I mentioned Hamstersaurus Rex. They snickered when I brought up Squirrel Kong.

Dylan—her right knee tightly wrapped in a massive clump of unneces-sary bandages—tried to be positive. She came up with a crazy plan to obtain a similar-looking hamster from the local pet store and somehow swap it out for Hammie at the last second. But I wasn't about to let another inno-cent hamster go down

for Squirrel Kong's crimes. Besides, where were we going to find a second hamster with a dinosaur tail and fangs?

The final school bell rang to go home. Time was up. But there was still one place I had yet to investigate.

"You sure you want to do this?" whispered Dylan. "Principal Truitt made it super clear that nobody is supposed to be poking around in here."

She scanned the hallway. It was empty. Pretty much everyone had gone home by now, but I knew from experience that Mr. Grogan might happen by any second with his bucket and mop. We didn't have much time.

"No choice," I said. "If I don't do *something*, then I may never see Hammie Rex again. But I totally understand if you want to back out now."

"No way," said Dylan, holding up her fist. "I stand with Hammie."

I nodded, and we started to pull aside the many layers of yellow caution tape that blocked the entrance to Room 117.

Inside it was dark and eerie. Random planks had been crudely nailed over the hole in the wall, giving the science lab the feeling of a zombie movie right before an undead attack. We replaced the caution tape as best we could and I flicked on the light of my UltraLite SmartShot to guide our way.

The devastation was total. Lab tables had been smashed to splinters. The glass of shattered beakers crunched underfoot. It looked like someone had gone for an indoor joyride in a tank. I needed something that definitively proved that this had been caused by a giant squirrel, not a dino-hamster. But what?

"Hey, look at this," said Dylan, picking up a crumpled piece of paper off the floor. "I got an A on the quiz about cell division."

Sure enough, the name at the top read "Dylan D'Amato" with a score of 9/10.

"Heh," said Dylan. "Looks like I only missed the question about cytoplasm."

I noticed something strange about the paper. It had a weird orange splotch on the corner.

"What is that stuff?" I asked.

"Oh," said Dylan, reading, "Cytoplasm is 'C.' The gelatinous material that fills the inside of eukaryotic cells—'"

"No, no, that orange stuff."

"Huh. No idea. Ew," said Dylan, seeing that she'd gotten a little on her fingers. She wiped it off on her jeans. "Sam, you've got some on your elbow."

Sure enough, I had a splotch on my shirtsleeve. I sniffed it. I couldn't quite place it, but there was something familiar about the smell.

As I shone the light around, I now saw that smudges of the same orange dust were everywhere in the science lab: on a broken chair, on a smashed light fixture, on a biology textbook with a giant chomp taken out of it, on a flattened test tube rack—

Hang on. A textbook with a giant chomp taken out of it?

I picked up the book. It was thickly coated with the orange dust and the bottom third was missing. A single, perfect bite had been taken out of it. You could see the outline of every tooth.

"Check this out," I said. "There's no way Hamstersaurus Rex could have taken a bite like this."

"You're right. You'd need a mouth a foot wide to do that," said Dylan, examining the book for herself. "Still, you can't necessarily *prove* that a giant squirrel did it. You'd need to be an expert in—"

Just then, we heard the sound of footsteps outside in the hallway.

"Somebody's coming," hissed Dylan.

We froze, and I killed the light on my camera. Now the lab was dark once more. The footsteps got louder. Someone was approaching the door to Room 117.

"Hide!" I whispered.

Dylan nodded and dove behind an overturned desk. I scrambled into a cabinet with a broken door.

From my vantage point, I could still see the doorway. A tall silhouette was now outlined through the layers of yellow caution tape. I caught the flash of metal as something poked through. Snip. A layer of tape fell away. Snip. Another fluttered aside. Someone was cutting their way inside with a pair of scissors. Once they'd cut the last strand, the mysterious figure stepped into the room.

CHAPTER 7

I HELD MY BREATH and watched the figure gingerly take another step into the lab. Something cracked under their shoe. I could see now that it was a man wearing a white lab coat. Beyond that I couldn't make out many details, but something about him seemed . . . familiar. He felt his way along the far wall, right toward Dylan's hiding spot. I held my breath and hoped he didn't step on her.

He didn't. He turned on the lights.

"Whoa!" screamed the man, leaping back three feet as he saw Dylan lying on the floor. "Very uncool!"

"Uh. Hi," said Dylan.

With the lights on, I instantly knew where I'd seen him before. He had the same ponytail, the same gratuitous indoor sunglasses. He was the double thumbs-up guy from the principal's office.

"Yo, like, what are you even *doing* in here?" said the man, panting.

"What am I even doing in here?" said Dylan, standing and dusting herself off. "What am I even doing in here? What am I even doing in here? Uh, Sam, what am I even doing here?"

"I am not Sam," I said in a heavy accent as I squeezed out of my cabinet.

The surprised man screamed again.

"I am his identical cousin Jarmo, from Finland!" I said, "We were playing a very much fun game called *piilosta laboratorio*—where you hide in a scientific lab for great joy. You just won the game by finding us! A hundred and fifty congratulations to you."

"Yep, that's right," said Dylan, nodding rapidly. "A hundred and fifty congratulations to you, sir. I'm, uh, from Finland, too. Even though I, uh, can't do the accent—I mean, I don't *have* an accent."

"You're from Finland, too?" said the man. "So what's your name?"

Dylan frowned. "My Finnish name?"

The man nodded.

"It's Finnn . . . Fin," said Dylan.

"Your name's 'Finfin'?"

Dylan nodded. I face-palmed.

The man's expression softened. "Look, homies," he said. "You don't have to make a bunch of crazy junk up. I get it. You two were poking around where you shouldn't be and you got caught by the quote unquote 'Man': me."

Dylan and I looked at each other.

"Yeah," we said in unison.

The man picked a miraculously unbroken chair up off the floor and set it on its legs. Then he spun it around backward and sat down in it.

"Mind if I rap with you a little?" he said.

"No," I said. "We don't mind if you rap with us."

"Real talk," he said. "I get it. I was young once, too. And trust me, nobody was a bigger trouble-maker than me. In fact, I used to cut class all the time to ride skateboards and play bass and do bungee jumping."

"That sounds pretty awesome," said Dylan.

"If you think being a rebel who plays by his own rules is awesome." The man shrugged. "Anyway, the name's Duderotti. Todd Duderotti. I'm your new science teacher."

"Welcome to Horace Hotwater Middle School," said Dylan.

Mr. Duderotti held out his fist. Dylan bumped it.

"Look, I'm not going to narc on you for being in the lab or whatever," said Mr. Duderotti. "But I guess since I'm a so-called 'authority figure,' I should probably tell you: it would be totally un-rad if you ever did something like this again. I mean, look at all the broken glass and exposed wires and junk. You little dudes could really hurt yourselves."

"We understand," I said. "We're very sorry. It won't happen again, Mr. Duderotti."

"Please, Mr. Duderotti was my old man. Call me Todd."

"We understand, Todd," I said. It didn't sound right as I said it.

"Okay," said Mr. Duderotti, standing. "Great rap session. I'll see you both in school tomorrow. We're going to be learning the difference between plant cells and animal cells." He pantomimed a little air-guitar riff.

Dylan smiled.

"Remember," said Mr. Duderotti, pointing at us, "knowledge is the original rap music."

"I'll try to remember that," I said.

He held out his fist to me. Somewhat reluctantly, I bumped it. Over Mr. Duderotti's shoulder, I saw Dylan quickly swipe the chomped book and hide it behind her back. We both hurried out the door.

"Stay chill, amigos," called Mr. Duderotti after us, and he made a sort of "hang loose" gesture with his hand. Dylan waved.

"Wow, what a nice guy," said Dylan, once we'd made it out of earshot. "I can't believe he's going to let us call him by his first name."

"He didn't seem a little off to you?" I said.

"He only seemed off to you, Sam, because he's cool."

"Wait, are you implying that I'm not cool?" I said. "Because I'm cool. I'm really cool. Have you seen my dioramas?"

"Look, we could debate your coolness level all day long, but I've got to get to practice," said Dylan. "Weekes's inner peace is going to turn into outer rage when he sees me drag in twenty minutes late." She tossed me the book. "But you finally have your evidence: tooth marks that might have been made by Squirrel Kong."

"They were!" I said. "But I'm going to need help from someone who's an expert in rodent dental forensics."

Oddly enough, I knew someone like that.

Fifteen minutes and a quick phone call to my mom later ("Meeting Club is running long today! So much lively debate!"), I was on the crosstown bus. The sky overhead was dark and ominous. It felt like a downpour might start at any second.

As the bus pulled over at my requested stop, I could see the gleaming SmilesCorp campus on a hill in the distance.

"You sure this is where you want to get off, kid?" said the bus driver. "You know this museum is just a bunch of spooky old dolls, right?"

"All too well," I said as I hopped out of the bus and ran toward the Antique Doll Museum. Outside, I saw Martha's tandem bicycle locked up.

"We're closed," said Patricia, the ticket taker.

"No, you're not," I said, pointing to the sign of posted hours. They were clearly open for another forty-five minutes.

"Fine. You called my bluff. It was worth a shot," she said with a shrug. "Five dollars."

I slapped a bill on the counter and rushed for the entrance. Unfortunately, I was so distracted I didn't see that a woman was coming out of the same door at exactly the same time. I bumped into her and she dropped an armload of papers on the ground.

"I'm really sorry, ma'am," I said as I stooped to help her pick up her things. "I guess I wasn't thinking there would be any other, you know, *people* here."

"Don't be sorry," said the woman. "We're always glad to see a new patron! I'm the new PR director at the museum and I have to ask. Were you attracted by our new ad campaign, 'The Maple Bluffs Antique Doll Museum: Absolutely Doll-icious'?"

"Um. No?" I said, handing her a stack of papers. I was surprised to see Roberta Fast— the SmilesCorp rep who had lost the company's invisible doughnut at Science Night—staring back at me.

"Hey, I know you!" said Roberta, smiling. "Sam Gibbs, winner of the Little Mister or Miss Muscles competition."

"I cheated," I said with a shrug. "Wait, I thought you worked at SmilesCorp?"

Roberta Fast's face darkened. "Not anymore," she said. "I just couldn't do it. I got sick and tired of the soulless corporate atmosphere; the lies; the unethical behavior. It was too much. So I quit. I'm telling you, Sam Gibbs, that company is evil. And so are all the people who thoughtlessly help their foul agenda of seeking profits at any cost!"

"My mom still works there, so . . . ," I said.

"Oh, she's fantastic! One of the good ones!" said Roberta Fast, instantly brightening again. "And how's your pet hamster? The one that caused all that adorable property damage? The little guy is doing well, I hope!"

"Not really; the principal of my school wants to send him to hamster prison," I admitted. "Anyway, it was, uh, nice to run into you, Ms. Fast. Congrats on the new job."

"Don't be a stranger," said Roberta. "And next

time be sure to enter the offer code 'DOLLICIOUS' when you buy your tickets online for a forty-five-cent discount."

"Will do," I said.

And with that, Roberta Fast walked out into the parking lot toward her silver hatchback. I continued onward, past shelf after shelf of the dustiest, creepiest dolls history had to offer. Norton, the security guard, doffed his cap as I walked past.

I found Martha Cherie stuffing a wad of suggestions in the museum's Suggestion Box. She wore a blue blazer and a gold lapel pin, marking her as an official Antique Doll Museum intern.

"Oh, hello, Sam," she said. "Are you here to check out the Fanged Dolls of Medieval Hungary exhibit? It's closing next weekend."

"No, Martha," I said. "I need your help."

"That's what I'm here for!" She pointed to her

lapel pin. "Just let me finish adding my daily suggestions to the Martha Suggestion Box. I used to say all my suggestions about how the museum could be better run out loud, to the museum staff, and that's why they added the box. It's just for me. Can you imagine, a whole box filled with my thoughts!"

Martha stuffed eight more suggestions into the slot. The box was so full that the last one barely fit. She scribbled on a final slip of paper and narrated as she wrote: "Need bigger Martha Suggestion Box." She left that one sitting on top.

"Now, what did you want help with, Sam? Is it navigating our vast collection of loose doll arms on the third floor? I'm afraid it can be a tad daunting to patrons who are new to the exciting world of doll arms, but with a little guidance, I think you'll find it a very rewarding experience."

"Not doll arms," I said. "Look, you remember how I told you that a giant squirrel attacked our school?"

Martha frowned. "Yes," she said. "Even though we're friends, I thought that claim sounded outlandish and unbelievable. I've noticed you're sometimes prone to mendacity. Which means 'lying.'"

I pulled the chomped book out of my backpack and handed it to her.

"Well, I'm not lying about this," I said. "You see those tooth marks? They were made by Squirrel Kong."

Martha stared at the book. For an instant I thought I saw a hint of something flash in her eyes. Then she handed it back to me. "It sounds like the help you're asking for doesn't involve antique dolls at all," she said, "but rather exonerating a certain type of rodent, which I'd rather not name."

"You can prove that that bite mark came from a twelve-foot-tall squirrel and not a hamster with fangs. You can use your rodent dental forensics to save Hamstersaurus Rex!"

"No, Sam," said Martha. "I left that world behind. I have a new life now. And unless one of these precious antique dolls gets gnawed by a ferret or something, rodent dental forensics doesn't play any part in it."

"But Hamstersaurus Rex is getting sent away tomorrow!" I said. "You're my last hope." I felt like crying.

"Sorry, Sam," said Martha, "but I'm not a Hamster Monitor anymore."

I took a deep breath. "Martha, you didn't leave the cage unlocked that day," I said. "I took Hamstersaurus Rex out for the night. It was my fault."

Martha stared at me in shock and disbelief. "What?"

"I should have told you sooner."

"And you just let me resign my post? Humiliate myself in front of the entire class? You let me think I *made a mistake?*" said Martha, her eyes wide. "Sam, I thought we were friends."

"We are! And that's why I need—"

"I *said* I'm not a Hamster Monitor anymore!" cried Martha, wiping a tear from the corner of her eye. "And guess what? I don't think you're one either!" Then she turned and walked away.

I felt awful. I'd managed to hurt Martha's feelings and failed to save Hamstersaurus Rex. Lost in thought, I walked out of the museum and crossed the parking lot toward the bus stop. The dark clouds overhead still threatened rain. I walked past a compact SUV and—

THUD! For the second time that day, I physically bumped into someone. To be fair, this time it wasn't really my fault. The person I'd collided with was crouched behind the back bumper of the vehicle, clutching a pair of binoculars and a strange hand-held technological device with a long wobbly antenna.

"Sorry!" I said, before I realized who it was— indeed, quite possibly the last person I'd ever want to see.

I'd walked right into Kiefer "Beefer" Vanderkoff.

CHAPTER 8

"**Y**OU'VE BEEN FOLLOWING me?!" I cried, leaping back in surprise.

"What? No way!" sputtered Beefer, hiding the binoculars and antennaed device behind his back. "I mean, maybe you've been, uh, following *me*!"

"Beefer, you're the bully who made my existence miserable for six long years," I said. "Why would I be following *you*?"

"Well, you and your psychotic attack gerbil completely ruined my life!" said Beefer. "So why would I be following *you*?"

"Huh? How's that?" I said. "I ruined *your* life?"

"You stole my girlfriend and got me kicked

out of school and forced me to smash my head against a trophy that was made of rocks!"

"I—*what?*" I said, dumbfounded.

"You think I've forgotten about what happened on Science Night?" said Beefer. "I haven't!"

"Why do you have those binoculars?" I cried. "What are you doing creeping around in the Antique Doll Museum parking lot spying on me? What's that weird antenna thingie you've got?"

"I don't owe you any answers," said Beefer, his expression hardening. "Just tell me where he is or I'll pummel your dumb nerd face."

"Over my dead body!" I said. I wasn't about to give up Hamstersaurus Rex's location to the likes of Beefer Vanderkoff.

"Works for me!" cried Beefer. "Anteater style!"

Beefer shifted into a strange martial arts fighting stance that, I grudgingly had to admit, did sort of look a little bit like an anteater. I tried my best to put up my own dukes while at the same time protecting my "nerd face." I wasn't really afraid of Beefer anymore, but he had a point: he definitely *could* pummel me. We circled each other warily.

"Before we fight, is there *any chance* you still believe I'm a werewolf?" I asked.

"Ha! I'm not that dumb," said Beefer. "I know you cured the curse by waiting till it was a full moon and fully submerging yourself in pure Dijon mustard."

"Seriously, man. *What?*"

"Anteater Takes the Ant!" cried Beefer as he lunged at me. I just managed to scramble back-ward out of his grasp.

Beefer resumed his fighting stance. "You know what I call you, man?" he said with an evil grin.

"What?"

"Sam *Dweebs!* Which is a *clever play* on your *stupid last name!*"

"Those two words don't even sound similar!" I cried in disbelief. "Oh, and Gibbs is a stupid last name but Vanderkoff isn't?"

"It's Duuuuuutch!" howled Beefer as he flew at me again, twirling both fists like some sort of double-anteater windmill.

A beefy arm caught him around the midriff and yanked him backward off his feet.

"All right, break it up!" It was Norton, the Antique Doll Museum security guard. "Break it up! No fighting in the parking lot!"

"Lemme go!" screamed Beefer, squirming in Norton's grip.

"You!" said Norton, recognizing Beefer now. "You fell on Ginny Gossamer, destroying history's most fragile doll! You have a lifetime ban from Antique Doll Museum property! You're not going anywhere until I call the police!"

With a powerful lurch, Beefer managed to wriggle out of Norton's grasp. He took off across the parking lot at top speed.

"None of you can stop me!" cried Beefer. "I have a master plan! And I swear I'll get him back if it's the last thing I do!" He took a running dive into the bushes.

By the time I made it to the edge of the lot, Beefer was long gone. I heard his tromping footsteps fading in the underbrush. There was no way I could possibly catch up to him. Norton arrived a moment later, completely winded.

"I will avenge you, Ginny Gossamer," said Norton, waving his fist.

I caught the crosstown bus heading in the opposite direction. The route would take me back past the school to the stop near my house. My encounter with Beefer had me thoroughly rattled. As I rode, I watched the storm clouds churn and wondered what he had to do with all of this. What was Beefer's master plan? His ominous parting words echoed in my mind: *I swear I'll get him back if it's the last thing I do.*

I cursed myself for not chasing him down. Beefer was obviously *still* obsessed with getting revenge on Hamstersaurus Rex. Not only did I have to stop a twelve-foot-tall squirrel and clear Hammie's name in the next fourteen hours—now I had to worry about Beefer, too.

Suddenly it dawned on me: this *was* Beefer's master plan. The giant squirrel attacks weren't random at all. Beefer was somehow controlling

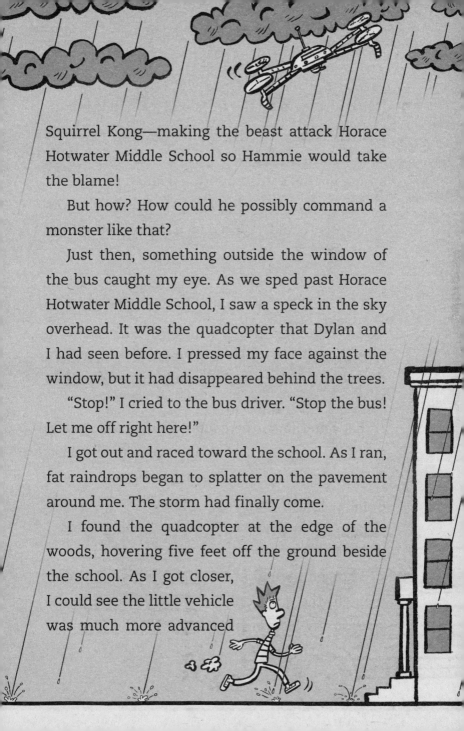

Squirrel Kong—making the beast attack Horace Hotwater Middle School so Hammie would take the blame!

But how? How could he possibly command a monster like that?

Just then, something outside the window of the bus caught my eye. As we sped past Horace Hotwater Middle School, I saw a speck in the sky overhead. It was the quadcopter that Dylan and I had seen before. I pressed my face against the window, but it had disappeared behind the trees.

"Stop!" I cried to the bus driver. "Stop the bus! Let me off right here!"

I got out and raced toward the school. As I ran, fat raindrops began to splatter on the pavement around me. The storm had finally come.

I found the quadcopter at the edge of the woods, hovering five feet off the ground beside the school. As I got closer, I could see the little vehicle was much more advanced than the cheap models you can purchase online. It had a camera on the front and a small mechanical grasping claw mounted to its undercarriage. Beside the grabby claw thingie, it also had a strange metal canister with a pointed nozzle.

I approached the quadcopter slowly now. As quietly as I could, I picked up a heavy stick off the ground.

Hisssssssss . . .

I froze. Now the purpose of the metal canister was clear: the copter was spraying something onto the outside wall of the school. It was more of the weird orange dust I'd seen in the science lab. Huh?

Back and forth the copter wove, methodically coating a large section of the wall with the dust. At last, the spraying stopped. The orange splotch it had created was the approximate size and shape of a large door. The quadcopter paused. I had one chance.

I lunged, swinging my stick overhand. At that moment the quadcopter randomly darted to the side, so my blow missed. My stick thudded into the dirt. The copter spun, and for a split second I looked right into the glass eye of the camera. Then the quadcopter zipped straight up into the sky and out of sight.

Lightning flashed. It was so bright and so close that I reflexively covered my eyes. An instant later thunder crashed, a deafening boom right overhead. I could practically feel my teeth rattle.

Rain was falling in sheets now, but the rolling rumble didn't stop. At first I thought my ears were still ringing. But then I realized it wasn't thunder. It was the sound of feet.

Lighting flashed again. In the darkness of the woods I saw a huge, shaggy beast barreling toward me. It was Squirrel Kong.

CHAPTER 9

KABLAM!

Like a fuzzy semitruck, Squirrel Kong smashed right through the wall of the school as easily as if it were made of papier-mâché. The beast burst through the exact spot where I'd been standing approximately fourteen milliseconds earlier. Somehow, I managed to fling myself out of the way before being pulverized.

Thunder crashed again. I landed on my stomach in the mud and lay motionless, too terrified to move. Nearby, Squirrel Kong hunched over the pile of loose bricks from the wall and made sickening slurping noises as it greedily licked the orange dust off the rubble.

The copter had sprayed the wall exactly where it wanted Squirrel Kong to attack! That's how Beefer was commanding the monster. The antennaed device I'd seen him holding must have been quadcopter's remote control.

Above me I heard a buzzing sound as the quadcopter made a rapid descent. It dropped to a few feet off the ground and then zipped through the hole that Squirrel Kong made, disappearing inside Horace Hotwater. Scared as I was, I felt a new surge of panic rising in my chest. The quadcopter was flying toward Principal Truitt's office. Beefer was going after Hamstersaurus Rex!

Overcoming my fear, I pushed myself up onto all fours and slowly started to crawl through the mud. Inch by inch, I made my way past Squirrel Kong—who ignored me as it continued to lick up the orange dust—and into the school. Once I'd put a few feet of distance between myself and the beast, I leaped to my feet and started to run. I had no idea what other unpleasant surprises Beefer's quadcopter had in store—buzz saw?

Flamethrower? Quad-laser?—but I knew I had to get to Hammie before it did. If I took a shortcut, I might just be able to beat it there.

I ran as fast as I could, ducked in one side of the auditorium, dashed down the aisle between the folding seats and out the other. I rounded the corner of the hallway to see the school office. But I was too late. The glass window of the reception area was smashed in. The whole area was eerily quiet.

"Hammie?" I called out. "Are you okay? I'm here to—"

The quadcopter zipped out of a window right at me. I stumbled backward, surprised, as it buzzed past my face. In its grasping claw it carried the PETCATRAZ Pro™ that held Hamstersaurus Rex!

"Hammie!" I cried.

I somehow managed to spin and hook my fingers through the bars of the cage. With all my strength I yanked the copter back and grabbed it with my other hand.

"Ha! Gotcha!" I cried. I held the quadcopter firmly.

Hammie Rex snarled from inside his cage, eager to smash, stomp, or chomp something.

The quadcopter twisted and turned in my grasp—surprisingly strong for its size—rotating its propellers this way and that. The grasping arm released its claw grip on the cage and flailed wildly. It seemed like the copter was only trying to escape now. But I had no intention of letting that happen. I spun it around so that I was facing the camera.

"Nice try, Beefer," I said right into the glassy camera. "But you messed with the wrong—"

PSSSSSSSHT! In a powerful burst, the quadcopter unloaded its remaining payload of pressurized orange dust right into my face. I choked and sputtered as I inhaled the sticky, savory stuff. In a coughing fit, I lost my grip on the copter.

The instant I let go, it was airborne again. It zipped off down the hallway and disappeared out of sight.

As I wiped my eyes and spat out gooey gobs of the orange dust, I finally realized what it was. There was no mistaking that taste—savory, tangy, utterly unlike anything found in nature—it was concentrated Funchos Flavor-Wedge flavoring!

I caught sight of my reflection in a window and blinked. From my head all the way down to my waist, I was completely orange, thoroughly coated in the stuff. I looked like a walking Flavor-Wedge! Inside his cage, Hammie Rex was even more agitated than ever, ricocheting around like a pinball.

"It's okay, little dude," I said as I knelt. "You're safe now. You don't have anything to worry about."

Just then, a bloodcurdling screech echoed through the school. I knew now that it was the war cry of Squirrel Kong. The following thoughts fired off in my brain in quick succession:

A. Squirrel Kong attacked anything coated in the orange dust.

B. Currently, *I* was coated in the orange dust.

C. *Therefore, run!*

I picked up the PETCATRAZ Pro™ and scrambled through the broken window into the school office reception area. Then I dropped to all fours and crawled toward the door marked "Principal Truitt," dragging the cage along behind me.

Once inside, I closed and locked Principal Truitt's office door. Then I huddled behind her heavy desk. Hammie continued to rage and snarl and foam at the mouth.

"Shhhh!" I pleaded, but he didn't listen.

Outside I heard a crash. Then another. Squirrel Kong was close. The door to Truitt's office would slow it down about as much as a layer of tissue paper. Our only hope was remaining hidden. Hamstersaurus Rex's noisy growling would make that impossible.

"Please, Hammie! I've told you before, you're no match for that thing!" I whispered. "We just have to hide! What do I have to do to keep you quiet?"

As soon as I said it, I knew. I threw open the lower left drawer of Principal Truitt's desk. Sure enough, it was still filled with bags of Spicy Wasabi and French Onion Flavor-Wedges. I tore open a bag and dumped it through the bars of Hammie's cage. The little guy started to gobble.

"That ought to hush you up for a few . . ."

But my heart sank as I saw the carpet behind me. Even if Hammie didn't make another peep, there would be no hiding. A series of orange dust splotches from where I had crawled across the floor led right under the door to the very spot where I was cowering. I'd stupidly left a Funcho flavoring Hansel and Gretel trail that Squirrel Kong could follow right to us!

As if to confirm this, there was another crash.

The monster was definitely inside the school office now and coming this way. I had to do something, fast. I looked around for anything that might help.

CRASH! The door to the principal's office blasted inward, practically disintegrating from a Squirrel Kong head-butt. With a crazed look in its eyes, the beast let out another terrifying squeak-howl.

It was now or never. I leaped onto the top of the desk. Momentarily surprised, Squirrel Kong blinked. Then I dashed across the room, carrying Hammie's cage and emptying the other nine bags of Flavor-Wedges onto the floor behind me as I went. I leaped over the Squirrel Kong's whipping tail and ran out the door.

For a moment, the giant squirrel was conflicted: Follow the human Flavor-Wedge or eat the ones on the floor? Behind me, I heard the beast noisily begin to feast. I'd bought myself a few seconds at least. Would it be enough?

I flew out of the school office and skidded right. If I could make it to the other end of the hallway, maybe I could get out of the main entrance of the school.

Another crash rang out behind me! Squirrel Kong was smashing its way through doors and furniture to get out of the school office. I turned to see the beast pause for a second in the hallway to sniff the air. Then it turned and started to gallop toward me, shaking the walls as it came.

I had a horrible realization: as long I was covered

in Funchos dust, Squirrel Kong would follow me anywhere. And Squirrel Kong was unbelievably fast. You know how fast a regular squirrel is? Well, it was like that but way bigger. The monster could easily outpace me, especially since I was lugging a heavy hamster cage with a very agitated Hammie Rex inside. I huffed and puffed and tried to speed up, but Squirrel Kong was gaining on me now. I wasn't going to make it out the door. I wasn't going to make it fifty more feet.

I tripped and hit the floor with both elbows. The PETCATRAZ Pro™ clattered against the linoleum. I flipped onto my back to see Squirrel Kong skidding to a halt, its massive head less than two feet away. It sniffed me again.

"Good Squirrel Kong," I whispered. "Nice Squirrel Kong. You don't want to eat me. I'm not a Flavor-Wedge, I promise."

Squirrel Kong wasn't persuaded. It loomed over me now, licking its chops. Drool dripped from its glistening teeth in sticky ropes. Hamster-saurus Rex roared uselessly. Squirrel Kong spread its jaws wide to devour me and—

KALANG!

Just as Squirrel Kong bit down, I flung the entire PETCATRAZ Pro™—with Hammie still inside!— right into the monster's gaping mouth. The whole cage compressed under the unbelievable force of the chomp. The bars bulged outward but . . . they didn't break, just as I knew they wouldn't. After all, the PETCATRAZ Pro™ is the strongest small rodent cage on the market. (Okay, I was only, like, 99 percent sure the bars wouldn't break, but please don't tell Hamstersaurus Rex that.)

Squirrel Kong shrieked in pain—it can't feel nice to bite down on a couple of pounds of high-grade titanium—and reeled backward. Its whipping tail took out a water fountain, sending it spiraling down the hallway and causing water to spray from the burst pipe. I snatched the cage and I was on my feet again, running. I had to keep going if I was going to save Hamstersaurus Rex.

I rounded a corner and glanced back over my shoulder. A crazed Squirrel Kong charged after me again. Suddenly I saw a classroom door swing open behind me. A ponytailed figure stepped out into the hallway and directly into the beast's path. It was Mr. Duderotti! The poor guy was going to get flattened by a monster squirrel before his first day of work. Ms. Becker was right: Our school wasn't safe at all. I wanted to yell out to warn him.

But before I could, Mr. Duderotti pulled something small out of his lab coat. It looked like an aerosol bottle.

"Not so fast," said Mr. Duderotti. He shook the bottle and then sprayed it right into the furry face of the oncoming giant squirrel.

Squirrel Kong froze in its tracks. The beast snorted and then began to scrabble wildly at its nose with its front paws. Mr. Duderotti stood his ground as the beast finally let out a booming sneeze. His lab coat and ponytail blew straight back like he was in a hurricane.

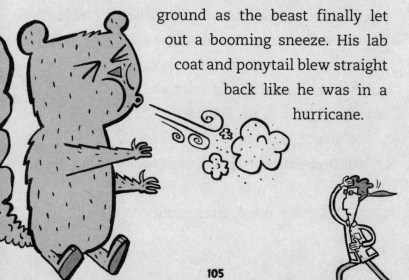

Then I saw the weirdest sight of my life. (The second weirdest was when Jared Kopernik tried to feed mashed potatoes to his own shadow.) Right before my eyes, Squirrel Kong started to *shrink*, smaller and smaller, until the once-fearsome monster was merely the size of a normal squirrel. Astonished, I realized that now Squirrel Kong *was* a normal squirrel. The horrible creature that had haunted my nightmares now looked tiny and pathetic on the ground before Mr. Duderotti's shoes. It was now slightly smaller than an average-sized burrito.

Mr. Duderotti dove for Squirrel Kong. But the animal leaped out of the way. The panicked squirrel wove left, then right, then it squeezed into an air vent that had been knocked loose in all the commotion. I heard its little claws clattering against the metal of the duct as it disappeared into the bowels of the school.

"Whoa," I said.

Mr. Duderotti sat up. I ducked back behind the corner.

"Hello?" he cried from down the hall. "Is

somebody else here? You should come out now! Trespassing on school property after hours is very . . . un-dope."

I realized that Mr. Duderotti hadn't seen me. But he definitely saw (and defeated!) Squirrel Kong. A teacher as an eyewitness ought to be good enough to prove that the giant squirrel was real.

I took a deep breath and made a split-second decision. Before anybody got the wrong idea about why I was here—during a Squirrel Kong attack that had demolished half of Horace Hotwater Middle School—I made a run for it.

CHAPTER 10

"**L**OOK, MY MOM says you shouldn't be bothering us this late," said Dylan, already talking before she opened the door. "We're not going to sign whatever it is you want us to sign or donate to whatever it is that you want us to donate to because it's dinnertime . . ."

Dylan trailed off and her jaw dropped open as she realized it was no random solicitor but instead her best friend since preschool. I stood on the D'Amatos' front porch, filthy and bright orange from my head down to my waist, carrying a partially squashed PETCATRAZ Pro™, inside of which was a hyperactive Hamstersaurus Rex.

"Hi," I said.

"Oh boy," said Dylan, shaking her head. "You should come inside."

I did.

"Mom! Dad! Sam's here!" bellowed Dylan as she hurried me upstairs to her room.

"Hiya, Sam," called Mrs. D'Amato from the kitchen.

"Hello, Mr. and Mrs. D!" I yelled back from the staircase.

"Want some dinner?" called Mr. D'Amato. "We're making soup!"

"Nah, I'm not hungry!" I called back. "Thanks, though!"

Hamstersuarus Rex roared.

There was a long pause from the kitchen. "You *sound* hungry," called Mrs. D'Amato.

"Okay, I guess I'll have a little soup," I answered.

Once we were inside Dylan's room, she slid a heavy wooden toy chest in front of the door.

"Got to make sure the room is little-brother proof," she said. She had three of them—Anthony, Pete, and Joey—so she always had to be on guard for whatever they had in store.

"Still, sometimes it must be *kind of* cool to have siblings," I said, sitting down on her bed and then immediately jumping back up as I remembered my Funcho dust coating.

"Does this look cool?" said Dylan. She held up her hairbrush. Its bristles were clogged with spaghetti. "But enough about the D'Amato family. Why are you orange?"

I told her everything that had happened since we parted ways at the end of school. She had trouble wrapping her brain around the idea of a remote-controlled quadcopter spraying Funchos dust in order to target a Squirrel Kong attack. She perked up at the Mr. Duderotti parts, though.

"Todd does seem like a pretty awesome guy," said Dylan after I'd described his heroic Squirrel Kong showdown.

"I guess," I said. "I mean, he really stood his

ground against a giant squirrel. Like, he had no fear. Didn't even flinch."

"To go bungee jumping, like Todd said he does, you pretty much *have* to be fearless," said Dylan.

I was detecting a certain awestruck quality in Dylan's attitude toward Mr. Duderotti—or "Todd," as she kept insisting on calling him.

"I wonder what was in that aerosol bottle," I said.

"Well, he's the science teacher, so maybe it was something he made with . . . science?"

"Really? He always keeps squirrel shrinking spray in his pocket?" I said. "Just in case?"

Dylan shrugged. "Sounds like it came in pretty handy," she said. "Anyway, what's with him?" She pointed to Hamstersaurus Rex. He was still frothing at the mouth, pupils dilated, growling and flinging himself around inside his cage. In short: rampaging.

"I honestly have no idea," I said. "He's been like this since I got sprayed by Beefer's stupid quadcopter."

"Is there anything we can do to calm Hammie

Rex down?" said Dylan. "Hot towel? Herbal tea? World music?"

"Got any Mint-Caramel Choconobs?" I asked. "Maybe some Spicy Cheez Wallets?"

"No way," said Dylan. "My mom doesn't let that stuff within three hundred yards of this house."

"Come on, little guy," I said as I moved to unlock the cage. "Just chill out." Hammie Rex snarled and went for my finger. I yanked my hand back and heard his jaws snap.

"It's your dust coating," said Dylan. "Hammie loves the taste of Funchos Flavor-Wedges the most, right? Forget Cheez Wallets, he probably wants to eat *you*."

"Just like Squirrel Kong," I said. "Can I go rinse off?"

On my way to the bathroom I found Joey D'Amato (age eight) sitting in the hallway filling a balloon with peanut butter and nickels.

"Why are you orange?" he asked.

"Why are you filling a balloon with peanut butter and nickels?" I asked.

He answered by lobbing the peanut-butter-

and-nickels balloon at my head. I ducked and it hit Anthony D'Amato (age six) right in the face, exploding everywhere. Anthony charged and tackled Joey. A second later, Pete D'Amato (age three and a half) came running and piled onto the brawl. Once again, I instantly appreciated being an only child.

In the bathroom, I washed the sticky Flavor-Wedge dust off in the sink, leaving orange trails all down the sides. Once I was clean, Dylan lent me a spare disc golf jersey to wear.

"Okay, let's try this again," I said as I cautiously unlocked Hammie Rex's cage. The little guy stomped forward and nuzzled my hand and then chomped my finger, but not as hard as he had tried to before. Hammie Rex was back to his usual not-insane self. Well, not *very* insane.

"That's better," I said as I took him out and scratched his scaly little back.

"Well, isn't that a happy ending to this whole thing," said Dylan.

"What do you mean?" I said.

"Squirrel Kong's done. And obviously Todd can confirm that a giant monster squirrel really *was* attacking our school like you said. So Hammie Rex's good name has been cleared and he won't get sent to that Indiana hamster home after all."

"I hope you're right," I said. "But somehow I don't think it's over."

"Why not?"

"Because," I said, "Beefer Vanderkoff is still out there."

CHAPTER 11

I ARRIVED AT SCHOOL the next morning with Hamstersaurus Rex hidden in my pocket. I immediately saw that Horace Hotwater had been even more badly damaged than I'd realized. Aside from the gaping hole in the wall and the busted water fountain, the school office had been completely trashed. Whole sections of the building were now blocked off with yellow caution tape that had the words "ANIMAL CONTROL—DO NOT CROSS" printed on it.

As I walked to my locker, I saw Martha headed in the opposite direction. She was reading what looked like a competitive origami manual.

"Martha, you'll never believe what happened after I left the doll museum!" I said. "Squirrel Kong got all shrunk down but I *still* have to stop Beefer because—"

"Honestly, I think you've done enough," said Martha, and she kept on walking. "Anyway, I'm pretty busy right now."

I sighed. She was still angry.

At the sixth-grade lockers, all the other kids were talking about the destruction.

"I can't *believe* Hamstersaurus Rex struck again," said Caroline Moody, shaking her head. "When will our long, school-wide nightmare ever be over?"

"Somebody's got to take that psycho hamster down," said Jimmy Choi, crossing his arms.

"It wasn't Hamstersaurus Rex," I said, tossing my bag into my locker.

"Yeah, sure. Of course you'd say that, Sam," said Jimmy Choi. "It's almost like you *want* your best buddy to destroy the school."

"Honestly, you guys have no idea what happened," I said. "This was another attack by—"

I caught myself before I mentioned Squirrel Kong. I was tired of being laughed at. "Whatever. Everyone will learn soon enough."

"Well, I heard Principal Truitt is calling an assembly first thing today," said Tina Gomez, "to talk about the incident."

"Great," I said. "Finally the truth will come out."

"I still think it was ghosts," said Jared Kopernik.

We all turned to stare at him.

"I heard this place was built on an ancient ghost burial ground," he said ominously.

The first bell rang, and just as Tina predicted, the entire school filed into the auditorium for the assembly. Dylan took a seat beside me.

On the stage, Principal Truitt looked both more frazzled and angrier than ever. Mr. Duderotti stood behind her looking cool with his arms folded behind his back. As always, he was wearing his indoor shades. Beside him stood a tall thin woman and a short fat man, both

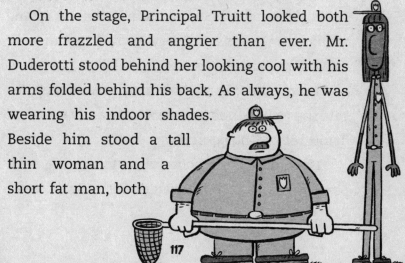

117

in identical khaki shirts.

"All right, settle down, everyone," said Principal Truitt, waiting for the buzz of conversation to die. "First off, we've had enough bad news recently, so I am determined to start this assembly off with something positive. In that spirit, I'd like to introduce all of you to Ms. Becker's replacement. Please give a warm Horace Hotwater Horace Hotwelcome to your new sixth-grade science teacher, Mr. Todd Duderotti."

The audience gave lukewarm applause as Mr. Duderotti stepped forward.

"Thanks, Elaine," he said. Principal Truitt winced. Her first name had never been revealed to us.

"I'd just like to say how stoked I am to be a part of this rad school," said Mr. Duderotti, giving a quick air-guitar riff. "Very excited to jam with all you little dudes: education style!"

Dylan grinned and gave him a thumbs-up. He returned a little nod and stepped back as Principal Truitt retook the podium.

"Now, on to less cheerful matters," she said. "Last night, Horace Hotwater Middle School was attacked by a destructive, possibly criminally insane rodent . . ."

I glanced around at the faces of my classmates. At last, Principal Truitt would confirm the existence of Squirrel Kong. I would no longer be a laughing-stock. Maybe this was a happy ending after all.

"That rodent's name," said Principal Truitt, "is Hamstersaurus Rex."

I sat bolt upright in my seat. I looked at Dylan. She stared back at me, wide-eyed, and shrugged. I tried to catch Martha's attention but she ignored me. Farther down the row, Caroline and Jimmy were looking at me with smug I-told-you-so faces.

Principal Truitt continued. "At around six p.m. yesterday evening, Hamstersaurus Rex apparently used his immense strength to burst out of the cage in my office. He proceeded to devour six pounds of Funchos Spicy Wasabi and French Onion Flavor-Wedges before cutting a swathe of destruction through the school and ultimately escaping by smashing through the outer wall."

What? That wasn't how it happened at all! I shifted in my seat and waited for Mr. Duderotti to speak up. He didn't. Instead he checked his cuticles.

"This aggression will not stand," said Principal Truitt. "I will not tolerate a climate of fear. I will not compromise the safety of my students. From here on out I am considering this dangerous, rogue hamster to be our school's public enemy number one!"

This couldn't be happening! Why wasn't Duderotti saying anything? Squirrel Kong had almost crushed him. Without his word, I had no way to prove that Hammie Rex wasn't guilty.

"This morning I notified the Maple Bluffs Department of Animal Control," said Principal Truitt. She beckoned and the khaki-shirted pair stepped forward.

"Hello, kids, I'm Special Agent Anne Gould," said the thin woman.

"And I'm Special Agent Ralph McKay," said the fat man.

"Rest assured we are trained professionals," said Gould, "with the expertise to deal with a situation like this."

"We're the agents who dealt with the escaped

pig that was knocking over all the mailboxes last year," said McKay. "Cover story of last June's *Animal Control Monthly*. We have copies if anybody's interested."

The crowd was quiet.

"More to the point," said Gould, "if any of you see Hamstersaurus Rex, you should consider him extremely dangerous. Do not approach him. Do not catch his attention. Call us or find a teacher or a staff member and notify them immediately."

"We've found that rewards work incredibly well to help citizens come forward in animal fugitive situations like these," said McKay. "Therefore, anyone who provides information that leads to the capture of Hamstersaurus Rex will receive this." He held up a check. "Three hundred dollars, courtesy of the Maple Bluffs Department of Animal Control."

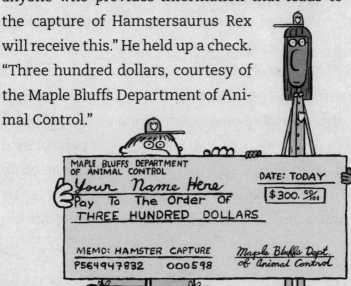

MAPLE BLUFFS DEPARTMENT
OF ANIMAL CONTROL

Pay To The Order Of *Your Name Here*

DATE: TODAY

$300.⁰⁰⁄₁₀₀

THREE HUNDRED DOLLARS

MEMO: HAMSTER CAPTURE

P564947832   000598

Maple Bluffs Dept. of Animal Control

Both agents nodded in unison and stepped toward the back of the stage. An excited murmur ran through the collected student body. Not only was the law on Hammie's trail; now, the prospect of a reward had turned every kid in school into a hamster bounty hunter. It wasn't supposed to go like this. Not at all.

Principal Truitt addressed the crowd once again. "Personally I find the timing of Hamstersaurus Rex's escape—the very night before he was to be sent away for good—to be highly suspicious. Know that anyone who is found to be aiding or abetting Hamstersaurus Rex in any way will face extremely serious consequences."

Her eyes scanned the crowd until she found me. I sank lower in my seat.

"Extremely. Serious. Consequences," repeated Principal Truitt, glaring at me. "Now, as I began this assembly on a positive note, I would like to conclude it on one. A SmilesCorp representative contacted me, and the company has generously agreed to donate the money needed to repair our school from this latest devastating attack.

We're so lucky to have them as a force for good in our community. Everyone, let's give a round of applause for SmilesCorp."

The crowd clapped wildly. I could tell that it wasn't some corporation's philanthropic efforts they cared about. The kids were amped up to get their hands on that sweet hamster reward money.

"Do you know how many snails you could buy with three hundred dollars?" I heard Wilbur Weber whisper to the person beside him.

My heart raced. At that very moment, Hammie Rex was hidden in my pocket, fast asleep.

"Now," said Principal Truitt, "that concludes our assembly. Please don't hesitate to—"

A deafening crash from outside cut her off. There was general confusion in the auditorium. The crowd began to murmur. Principal Truitt hurried off in the direction of the noise, quickly followed by Agents Gould and McKay. The teachers whispered among themselves. Gradually they began to take their classes back to their rooms.

As Mr. Copeland's sixth graders filed out of the auditorium, I saw a crowd of kids with their noses pressed against the window of the school. They were staring out toward the parking lot. I stood on my tiptoes to get a better look.

Out in the lot, Principal Truitt stood beside her car, an expensive black luxury sedan. Only it wasn't an expensive black luxury sedan anymore. It had been crushed flat. Its tires were folded out to the side like the legs of an old dog. Principal Truitt shook her fists with rage as Gould talked on her phone and McKay began to cordon off the area with more yellow tape. Even from far away, I could see that the vehicle was covered in telltale orange splotches.

Squirrel Kong was back.

CHAPTER 12

AFTER THE ASSEMBLY, the hallway was crowded with middle schoolers slowly making their way back toward their classrooms. I was terrified that someone would figure out that Hammie, now worth a cool three hundred bucks, was dozing in my shirt pocket.

I overheard Caroline Moody talking to Jimmy Choi. "I can't *believe* Hamstersaurus Rex smashed the principal's car while she was literally warning us about Hamstersaurus Rex," said Caroline. "He's got to be the most vengeful hamster who ever lived!"

"Maybe the *only* vengeful hamster that ever lived?" said Jimmy. "I mean, can you think of any other hamsters that have ever sought revenge? I can't name a single one."

"Guys, that's not what happened," I muttered, despite myself.

Jimmy and Caroline scowled at me.

"Oh, it isn't?" said Omar Powell, sidling up to me as we walked. "Are you saying that because maybe you know something we don't, Sam?"

I froze. Had Omar somehow figured out that the little guy was approximately two feet away from him, concealed behind the thinnest layer of plaid flannel? My hand reflexively crept up to my pocket. Luckily Hammie was still sleeping.

"Look, you know the most about Hamstersaurus Rex," said Omar. "Just tell me where he is and I'll give you two-fifteenths of the reward money. Minus my commission, of course. Eleven percent is standard."

"I honestly have no idea," I said. "Come on, why would you think I have any special insight into where he's hiding?" The pitch of my voice rose an octave as I finished the sentence.

"So *that's* how you want to play it, Sam?" said

Omar, cocking his head. "Fine. I guess you don't want your fifty-three dollars and forty cents."

"Play what?" I sputtered. "I'm not playing anything! I hate playing! I'm a very serious guy!"

"Never mind him, Sam," said Tina Gomez, edging Omar out, "I'm not going to ask you where Hamstersaurus Rex is hiding. I respect you way too much for that."

"Good," I said. "Thank you, Tina. That's very—"

"Just say the first *letter* of the place where he's hiding," said Tina.

"Tina, I'm not going to—"

"Is it an A?"

"What? No!" I said.

"Is it a B?"

"You can't just go through all the letters because—because I don't even know!"

"If he's hiding in Mrs. Gill's room, say no," said Tina.

"No! I mean yes—I mean—"

Tina's eyes lit up and she gave a sly tap to the side of her nose. "Thanks, Sam. That's all I needed." She turned and started to walk, then jog, then sprint toward Mrs. Gill's classroom.

This was getting ridiculous. I had to find a safe place to hide Hammie Rex away for the rest of the day. My shirt pocket was just too risky. I broke off toward my locker. Back when Beefer still haunted Horace Hotwater, that was usually a safe enough place for Hammie to hang out between classes. But when I got there, I found Drew McCoy listening to my locker with a stethoscope.

"What are you *doing?*" I said.

"When I grow up I want to be a doctor," he said. Then he shrugged and walked away.

So my locker was out. I needed somewhere more private. I needed to get Hammie to Meeting Club headquarters.

The crowd was thinning now. I quickly made my way toward Room 223b, making sure that no one was following me. As I dashed around a corner, I nearly smacked into Julie Bailey.

"Hey, Sam, do you know what flavor of Funchos Hamstersaurus Rex prefers?" said Julie. "Is he a Texas-Style BBQ Shawarma fan? Or more of a Roast Turkey and Sour Ketchup kind of guy?"

"Why do you ask?" I said, taking a nervous step back.

She unzipped her backpack to reveal ten bags of Funchos Flavor-Wedges, all different flavors. My heart skipped a beat.

"I figure if I open one of these bags Hamstersaurus Rex is bound to come running, right?" said Julie. "And then I can claim the reward money and maybe put a down payment on a pony."

"You know what," I said, "that doesn't really sound like a good idea because Hamstersaurus Rex doesn't really like Funchos anymore. He hates them. And they're too salty and he has high blood pressure, so . . ." I sounded totally unconvincing, even to myself.

"Hmm. Well, I guess there's only one way to find out, right?" said Julie. "I think I'll stick with a classic: Tangy Honey Habanero."

She tore a bag open. I felt Hamstersaurus Rex stir.

"You know what, I'm pretty sure I saw Hamstersaurus Rex in Mrs. Gill's room!" I cried.

Without another word, Julie jogged off just

as a drowsy Hammie Rex poked his head out of my pocket, his little whiskers twitching for junk food. That was a close one. I made sure the coast was clear and then I opened the door to Room 223b.

"Okay," I said as I set Hammie down on a stack of copies of *Tapeworms: An Illustrated History.* "Hide here and please, please, please, please, *please* don't draw any attention to yourself. We can't afford a mistake right now. The stakes are too high."

Hammie Rex growled. I recognized the look in his eyes: he was still hungry for Funchos. The little guy just couldn't control himself around Flavor-Wedges.

"You need some self-discipline, dude," I said. "You have to free yourself from the cycle of junk food addiction."

He stared up at me, wide-eyed. He seemed to actually be listening.

"Now, listen to me very carefully.

130

Relax and take a deep breath. Breathe in."

I demonstrated.

"Breathe out."

I did.

"Breathe in."

Hamstersaurus Rex inhaled at the same time I did.

"Breathe out."

The little guy exhaled.

"You are a rock in the middle of the sea," I said in a calm and steady voice. "Be the rock."

Hammie Rex continued to breathe deeply.

"You have total control of your impulses. . . . A rock doesn't go crazy over Funchos Flavor-Wedges. . . . You are a rock. . . . A rock doesn't risk everything for the sweet taste of junk food. . . . Be the rock. . . ."

We continued like this for a couple of minutes as I worked my way through all the meditation techniques I remembered from Coach Weekes's self-control MP3. Hammie Rex looked like he might actually be getting closer to some sort of inner peace. The little guy was sitting calmly, his eyes half-closed.

Ever so slowly, I took a bag of Classic Italian Cheddar and Mayo Flavor-Wedges from my backpack.

"Okay," I said, "now I'm going to open this, and I don't want you to lose—"

With a deranged yip, Hammie Rex flung himself at the Flavor-Wedges, spraying slobber everywhere.

"You nearly got my thumb," I said. "That's *definitely* not what a rock would have done!"

In a second and a half, the Flavor-Wedges were gone. Hammie Rex licked his whiskers, temporarily satisfied.

"Hopefully that will at least tide you over," I said, shaking my head. "I'll be back for you at the end of school."

I closed the door behind me. The halls were nearly empty now as I hurried toward Mr. Copeland's room. Ahead of me, I saw Mr. Duderotti directing the other few stragglers toward their classrooms. I stopped running. Why hadn't Mr. Duderotti mentioned Squirrel Kong? I needed to find out.

"Hey, Mr. Duder—" I said. "I mean, hey, Todd."

"Yo, Sam," said Mr. Duderotti. "*Qué pasa*, little bro?"

He held out his fist. I had no choice. I bumped it.

"Todd, why didn't you speak up during the assembly?"

"I don't know," said Mr. Duderotti, looking ashamed. "You're right. I really should have."

"You could have let the whole school know the truth," I said.

"Don't worry," said Mr. Duderotti, "I'm sure I'll get another chance to tell everyone that the Electric Tugboats were the greatest rock band of all time."

"Wait, what?" I said. "No, I mean the truth about the giant squirrel."

"Giant Squirrel?" said Mr. Duderotti, stroking his chin and considering this. "I like their first album, but everything after that was pretty corporate. After Ronny left, it wasn't about the music anymore, you know?"

"Not a band!" I said, "The real, live giant squirrel. The one you sprayed with—"

"I hate to be 'The Man' again," said Mr. Duder-otti, cutting me off. "But it's really time for you to get to class. Remember: learning is like playing the bass . . . with your *brain*."

I came away from the interaction feeling more confused and frustrated than ever.

As the day wore on, other kids kept asking me if I knew where Hamstersaurus Rex was, if I knew where Hamstersaurus Rex would be or if I wanted to help them catch Hamstersaurus Rex and split the reward money. My locker was broken into three times before lunch.

"Sam, be honest," said Jared Kopernik as I walked past him in the cafeteria, carrying my tray. "How come nobody has ever seen you and Hamstersaurus Rex in the same room at the same time?"

"Jared, you've seen them together dozens of times," said Dylan with a sigh.

Jared leaned over and whispered in my ear. "Admit it. Sam Gibbs is your secret identity. You're Hamstersaurus Rex."

"Yep. You're right, Jared," I said, shaking my head. "You totally figured it out."

"I did?" he said, surprised. "Then, uh, stay right here while I get a teacher!" Jared dashed off to go claim the hamster bounty.

Dylan and I sat down together to eat our lunch. All the kids at the nearby tables were pretending to talk while they watched and listened to us.

"This is the worst," I whispered to Dylan through my teeth, trying not to move my mouth in case any of my classmates knew how to read lips.

"What?!" said Dylan in an overly loud voice. "Hamstersaurus Rex is hiding in the bottom of the dumpster behind school? That's crazy!"

No less than eight kids leaped up and immediately raced out of the cafeteria.

"Serves them right," said Dylan.

I had to laugh.

"Man, I really don't get what's up with Mr. Duderotti, though," I said. "He knows the truth. He could have pointed out that it wasn't Hammie that attacked the school. Why didn't he say he has the anti-squirrel spray to defeat Squirrel Kong?"

"He must have his reasons. Todd is the coolest."

"Is he?"

"Sure," said Dylan. "Remember when he told us how cool he was?"

"I guess," I said. "But him being cool isn't going to help me stop the real menace."

"I've been thinking," said Dylan. "So far you've been on defense. Maybe it's time to play a little offense?"

"You're right," I said. "It's time to bring the fight to Beefer."

The rest of the day was more of the same: more kids following me around, more subtle (and not-so-subtle) Hamstersaurus Rex questions, more half-truths and evasions from yours truly. After school I collected Hammie Rex from Room 223b, deposited him into my backpack, and took the bus home. Jimmy Choi, Caroline Moody, and four fourth graders who I'd never seen before all got off at my stop.

"Really?" I said as we all stood on the curb. "You're all getting off here today?"

"Yep. I've just always loved this neighborhood. It has cool . . . grass," said Jimmy. He pointed to some grass.

"So it's just a coincidence that this stop happens to be where I live," I said.

"Wait, you live here, Sam?" said Caroline, with fake surprise.

"Yep," I said, crossing my arms.

"That's so cool," said Caroline, "and so which one of these houses, specifically, would be yours?"

"The green one, over there," I said, pointing to the house three doors down from mine.

"Is that where you're going now?" said Caroline.

"Nah, I think I'm going to hang out here and enjoy my neighborhood's cool grass for a while," I said. Then I stood and waited for all the other kids to awkwardly disperse, one by one, in different directions. Once they were all out of sight, I quickly ducked into Mr. Greco's boxwood bushes. I crawled around back and then made my way through the adjoining backyards to my own.

My mom wasn't home yet, so I fed Hammie Rex a quick snack—a half pound of frozen cookie dough covered in nacho cheese—and then headed straight back out to the garage.

I knew what I had to do. I had to go to the source

of all of this trouble, the very den of evil itself. With Hammie Rex tucked into my shirt pocket, I put on my helmet, opened the garage door, and hopped onto my bike. Then I pedaled as fast as I could.

As I raced down the street through my neighborhood, I saw the astonished faces of the kids who had followed me home. Caroline Moody was hiding under the Padillas' birdbath. Jimmy Choi jumped out from behind a mailbox on the corner. The four mystery fourth graders had somehow all squeezed into a single recycling bin, which tipped over as they scrambled out of it. All of them ran along the sidewalk behind me, but they couldn't keep up. After five blocks, I lost them all.

I didn't stop pedaling until I'd reached the most vile, sinister address in the whole town of Maple Bluffs—a place that, if you'd asked me mere days before, I would have sworn I would never go, not in a million years. I stood on the lawn of 3223 Birchpoplar Way.

Perhaps that address doesn't sound like a nexus of cosmic evil. And the house in front of me certainly didn't look very different from the others around it. But it was. The proof was a single sinister word written on the welcome mat: Vanderkoff.

"All right, Hammie, this is it," I said. "If I can goad Beefer into confessing what he's done, then I can finally put a stop to this, once and for all."

I pressed Record on my UltraLite SmartShot camera and dropped it into my backpack.

"Test . . . test . . . test," I said, to make sure the camera was still picking up audio. It was. Perfect.

Hammie growled, ready for action.

"We should be prepared for anything," I said, "but if Beefer is keeping Squirrel Kong in his basement or something, we can't engage. It's a fight you can't win."

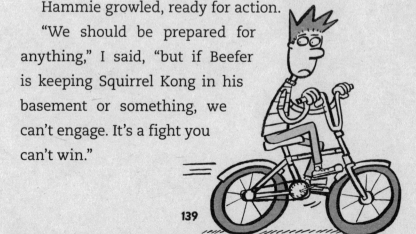

Hammie grunted in a way that sounded non-committal. I took a deep breath and then pressed the doorbell. Then I braced myself.

There was silence.

I heard movement inside. Someone was coming. I held my breath.

"Why, hello!" said a cheerful, smiling woman who, unfortunately, looked a whole lot like Beefer.

 **CHAPTER 13**

"**W**HERE'S BEEFER?" I said in a tone that instantly sounded too harsh.

"Whom?" said Mrs. Vanderkoff.

"Um. Kiefer, I guess," I said.

"Oh!" she said with a smile. "No need to be so formal. We always call him by his nickname: Lil' Kiefie. But Lil' Kiefie isn't home. He's having a sleepover with a new friend."

Beefer didn't have friends. It certainly sounded like a phony excuse for getting up to something.

"Are you a new friend of his, too?" asked Mrs. Vanderkoff.

"What?" I said, aghast. "Absolutely not!"

She cocked her head, confused.

". . . I mean, no way am I a *new* friend of, uh, Lil' Kiefie's," I said. "I actually know him from his old school, Horace Hotwater. We go way, way back." With Beefer gone, I realized, I might at least be able to poke around and gather some Squirrel Kong evidence.

"Well, isn't that sweet that you came to visit. My name is Judith Vanderkoff," said the woman, extending her hand. "I'm Lil' Kiefie's mother."

"I'm, uh, Jarmo," I said, shaking it. "But I'm *not* from Finland."

"Well, what a coincidence: Neither am I!" she said. "You should really come inside, Jarmo. We're having crumpets."

I stepped into the most florally patterned house I'd ever seen. I sat on a plastic-covered couch while Mrs. Vanderkoff served me tea and crumpets, which are basically like mini-pancakes. A happy-looking man in an extra-wide tie, who also unfortunately looked a whole lot like Beefer, soon joined us.

"Why, hello there, young fellow!" he said. "So you're a pal of Lil' Kiefie's."

"Yes, sir," I said. "We like to laugh and laugh."

"That's wonderful to hear," said Mr. Vanderkoff. "We sometimes worry that he studies too hard."

I nearly spat out my crumpet.

"We're both dentists and Lil' Kiefie says he wants to follow in our footsteps," said Mrs. Vanderkoff. "But privately, we're both hoping he continues to pursue his interest in Renaissance music."

"Renaissance music?" I managed to sputter.

"Why, yes," said Mrs. Vanderkoff, beaming. "He doesn't like to brag, but our Kiefer plays the lute like a magical little lute angel."

I swallowed very carefully so as not to choke.

"Mr. and Mrs. Vanderkoff," I said, "can I ask a serious question that may sound strange?"

"Absolutely, Jarmo," said Mr. Vanderkoff. "Anything for a friend of Lil' Kiefie's."

I took a deep breath. "Has Lil' Kieifie been keeping any oversized squirrels around here lately?"

The Vanderkoffs looked at each other. I studied their faces for any hint of recognition. They seemed baffled.

"Can't say as *I've* seen any oversized squirrels," said Mrs. Vanderkoff. "How about you, Julian?"

"Me neither, Judith. And I feel like I'd notice something like that," said Mr. Vanderkoff. "Why do you ask, Jarmo?"

"What? Oh, well, a bunch of us are planning a big . . . surprise party for Lil' Kiefie, and that's the, uh, theme."

"The theme is oversized squirrels?" said Mr. Vanderkoff.

I nodded.

"Well, I'm certain he'll just love it!" said Mr. Vanderkoff.

"Our son is certainly lucky to have a thoughtful,

considerate friend like you in his life, Jarmo," said Mrs. Vanderkoff.

"No, no, no. I'm lucky to have him in my life," I said, without even gagging. "Anyway, the real reason I came was that I was hoping maybe I could take a look around Lil' Kiefie's room . . . for a different reason . . . which is that he, uh, borrowed something from me. And that thing was . . . a shoe."

"Our son borrowed a single shoe from you?" said Mr. Vanderkoff, furrowing his brow.

"Yep," I said. "It's a very cool shoe."

"That certainly sounds like our Lil' Kiefie," said Mrs. Vanderkoff. "Style for miles."

Who were these people? How did they end up with Beefer Vanderkoff as a son?

"Here, let me show you to Lil' Kiefie's room," said Mr. Vanderkoff.

He stood and led me upstairs to a door on the second floor. It was covered in a massive poster depicting a werewolf in mid-explosion.

"Forgive us, Jarmo," said Mr. Vanderkoff. "Lil' Kiefie's room is a bit, um, untidy at the moment. Our son is intelligent, kind, and *extremely* handsome, but I hate to say it: he can be a little disorganized at times."

Mr. Vanderkoff opened the door a little. A noxious Beefer-like odor wafted out of the gap.

"Good luck finding that cool shoe, Jarmo," said Mr. Vanderkoff with a bright smile. He patted me on the back and then turned and disappeared downstairs, whistling.

I stepped into Beefer's room and shut the door behind me. Then I fumbled for the light switch.

As I turned it on I gasped. Calling the room "a bit untidy" was the understatement of the century. The entire floor was carpeted in a thick layer of dirty clothes, dirty dishes, and shredded Spicy Cheez Wallet bags. Empty cases of horror DVDs and broken karate-practice weapons were piled two feet high on the bed, which looked like it hadn't been made since before Beefer was born. A big, empty wood-and-wire-mesh cage sat in the corner, surrounded by melted candles and faded plastic flowers. It was a shrine to Michael Perkins, Beefer's pet boa constrictor. The walls of the room were totally papered with film posters with titles like *Blood Chunk, Welcome to Corpseville, The Mutant Beasts of Dr. Murder,* and *Barf Dracula II.*

I reached into my pocket, pulled out Hamstersaurus Rex, and gingerly set him down on the floor. Even Hammie looked grossed out by Beefer's natural habitat. He kept shifting from foot to foot, wrinkling his nose.

"I know it isn't pleasant," I said. "But we need to find something—stray squirrel hairs, quadcopter batteries, some sort of magic amulet that makes rodents grow—to prove Squirrel Kong exists and hopefully figure out Beefer's next move."

Hammie gave a determined little growl and then began to dig through the mess, flinging out old Choconob wrappers and greasy paper napkins and the occasional pair of underpants. Soon, the little guy completely disappeared underneath the thick floor coating of Beefer garbage.

Meanwhile, I checked the drawers of Beefer's nightstand. The bottom one was entirely full of illegal fireworks. The second drawer only contained used bandages. The top drawer was full of moldy hot dog buns. Blech.

It was like the world's most disgusting archaeological dig site. After fifteen minutes of searching, the most suspicious items I'd found were a beautiful cherry wood lute and an amateur guide to operating a ham radio. In short: ample evidence that Beefer Vanderkoff was a total weirdo, but no proof of any wrongdoing.

Just then I heard a growl from Hammie. The little guy had found something. I tromped through the mess to join him. Hamstersaurus Rex now stood on a big mound of dirty clothes and junk food wrappers in the corner. I took a deep breath and started to dig, too. Buried under the pile of Beefer's stuff, I had soon uncovered a scuffed wooden trunk. There was a heavy padlock on it.

"All right," I said to Hamstersaurus Rex. "Time for a dino-chomp."

Hammie opened his jaws wide and then bit down on the lock as hard as he could. With a metallic clang, it fell away in two pieces. I carefully opened the trunk.

It was completely full of Funchos Flavor-Wedges. Hamstersaurus Rex gurgled with glee. He had located Beefer's Flavor-Wedge stockpile.

"You always think with your stomach instead of your head," I said to Hammie Rex.

With a crazed look in his eyes, Hammie licked his chops and dove into the trunk. He started gobbling his way through the Flavor-Wedges. Under the dwindling orange pile of Funchos, something caught my eye. It was a small, leather-bound book. I reached in and picked it up. It looked like a journal of some sort. I brushed the orange flavor dust off it and cracked it open.

Sure enough, inside was Beefer's handwriting. Nearly illegible, the scrawls in the journal were so crabbed and tiny that I could barely make out what any of it said. As best as I could figure, it was pages upon pages of strange rants about bizarre, nonexistent animals. I saw a few handwritten URLs that were links to truthbusters.com, the crank conspiracy theory website that I'd run across when trying to find Squirrel Kong myself. Had Beefer lost his marbles? Toward the end, the journal turned into some sort of observation log with times and dates. Perhaps this was how he was planning the Squirrel Kong attacks?

I quickly flipped to the final page. It had today's date, with the following words:

My jaw fell open. Beefer's next Squirrel Kong attack was targeting SmilesCorp!

CHAPTER 14

"MOM, HE'S PLANNING something. Something big," I said. "And it's going down tonight!"

"Let me get this straight," said my mom. "You're saying that at the stroke of midnight, Kiefer Vanderkoff—the kid who broke a trophy over his head at Science Night—is going to somehow destroy SmilesCorp?"

"Yes!" I said. "He's making his 'final assault' on SmilesCorp Building Seven! Your coworkers could be in danger."

"First off, Building Seven is the accounting department," said my mom. "Does Kiefer hate numbers or something?"

"Probably!"

"Second, nobody will be around at midnight except security. And security is very, very tight. I go to SmilesCorp five days a week. We have armed guards and metal detectors and everything. I have to swipe my ID card just to get in the door! This Kiefer might be a tough sixth grader, but I'm certain that the SmilesCorp team can handle a twelve-year-old boy who, according to you, isn't even very bright."

"Okay, maybe he's *not* very bright," I admitted. "But it isn't just him we're talking about. Beefer has a remote-controlled quadcopter and a giant squirrel that can bust through walls!"

"Well, when you put it that way it certainly *does* sound serious. Should we call the president or go straight to the UN Security Council?" said my mom, an edge of sarcasm creeping into her voice.

"I *tried* calling the police," I said. "But the guy who answers the phone just hung up on me. He thought it was a prank call."

"Sam, I hesitate to indulge you, but what's your evidence for *any* of this?"

"I went over to Beefer's house earlier and I found his crazy master plan all written out in a pile of Funchos Flavor-Wedges."

"And did you tell Kiefer's parents what you think is going to happen?"

"Yes!"

"Then you've done your part."

"But they didn't believe me about any of it, either."

"Hmm. Yeah. I wonder why not," said my mom, cocking her head.

"They don't know what's going on," I said, throwing up my hands. "They're just nice people who don't understand that they've accidentally raised a monster in their own home!"

"If you told his parents that you think he's up to something, then that's all you can do," said my mom.

"You don't believe me, either," I said.

"Look, Bunnybutt, I love that you have such a powerful imagination. I love your drawings and

I love the movies that you've made. But there comes a point when you have to put that aside and deal with the real world."

"But that's what I'm trying to do!" I said. "The real world has giant squirrels in it!"

"Sam, this was fine when you were five or six," said my mom, "but you're really getting too old for this kind of thing."

So that was that. We ate dinner in silence. Beefer's parents weren't going to help me. The police weren't going to help me. My mom wasn't going to help me. After dinner, I called Dylan.

She sighed. "Man, I wish I could, but my parents are having a night out and I have to watch all three of my brothers. If I sneak out of the house, I'm liable to come back to a smoking crater. I'm really sorry, Sam."

"It's okay," I said. "Maybe I can persuade Martha."

"Oh. Yeah," said Dylan. "Good luck." She didn't sound hopeful.

I called Martha's house but nobody picked up. Maybe she wasn't home. Maybe she was still mad at me.

It was close to ten o'clock now, the traditional Sam Gibbs bedtime. I said good night to my mom, brushed my teeth, and climbed into bed. Then I waited until I could hear her snoring in her bedroom before I snuck back out to the living room, grabbed a few things, and stuffed them into my backpack. Then I made my way out to the garage. I still had one steadfast ally in my fight against the forces of darkness.

I opened the "Extension Cords" hypoallergenic habitat. Hammie Rex looked like he was ready for action.

"I know I won't be able to do this without you. You're my right-hand hamster."

He snarled in solidarity. I opened my shirt pocket and the little guy hopped in. Then I grabbed my bike and pedaled out into the night.

It was after eleven now. I rode through the dark and empty streets of Maple Bluffs toward SmilesCorp headquarters. Hammie Rex poked his head up to feel the cool night breeze on his furry little face. We were on a mission. I knew where and when Squirrel Kong would attack. If I was in the right place at the right time, I might be able to capture footage on my UltraLite SmartShot digital camera or maybe get a confession from Beefer— the proof I needed to exonerate Hammie Rex.

I'd been to SmilesCorp a few times with my mom over the years. Truthfully, the place had always kind of creeped me out. It was a series of ultra-futuristic office buildings in a wooded area on the edge of town, not far from the Antique Doll Museum. The SmilesCorp campus was surrounded by a huge deserted parking lot, lit at regular intervals by streetlights. I rode my bike between the buildings until I got to the one that displayed the number seven above its entrance. It was two stories tall, all smoked glass and brushed steel. Inside it was dark.

I hid my bike in the meticulously landscaped bushes. Then I crouched behind a bench that gave me a good view of the glass double doors that led into Building Seven. I switched my camera to night-vision mode. On the display, my dark surroundings now glowed eerie shades of vivid green. The digital clock on the display counted down the seconds. Hammie Rex sniffed quietly.

At 12:03 a.m. I saw a blur of movement on the camera. A dark figure crept along the wall of Building Seven. On the display I could tell—even though he was wearing a ninja mask—that it was Beefer Vanderkoff. Sure enough, he was clutching the quadcopter controller in his hand. I panned right and left. He seemed to be alone. No Squirrel Kong. Yet.

"All right, boy," I whispered to Hammie Rex, "sic him."

It was the moment Hamster-saurus Rex had been waiting for. He lit out at full speed toward Beefer, who was now trying to pick the lock of the main door of Building Seven with a playing card. Without a sound, Hammie Rex sprang into the air, spreading his jaws extra-wide.

7

Despite his ninja training or whatever, Beefer never saw the attack coming. An airborne Hamstersaurus Rex chomped down as hard as he could on Beefer's butt.

Beefer let out a high-pitched wail that sounded a bit like someone letting the air out of a blimp. Then he started to spin wildly. Hammie Rex held on fast, his teeth firmly sunk into Beefer's haunches.

"Gotcha, Beefer!" I cried, leaping to my feet. "This is a citizen's arrest. Stop right there."

Beefer didn't listen. A final bout of wild flailing managed to dislodge Hammie Rex.

"You're not going to get away with it," I cried, approaching with my digital camera in hand. "If you confess to everything, maybe you'll only get life in prison!"

Beefer took off. Hammie snarled and ran after him and I followed close behind. I watched Beefer disappear around the corner between Building Seven and Building Nine.

As I rounded the corner myself, I saw that he'd blundered into a dead end. A tall chain-link fence topped with barbed wire blocked the other end of the alley between the two buildings. Beefer was frantically trying to pull open the Building Seven service entrance, even though it required an ID. When he saw me, he froze and then shifted into his bizarre "anteater style" karate stance. Hammie Rex leaped in front of me, growling dangerously and baring his pointy Jurassic teeth.

"Consider your attack foiled," I said.

"My attack?" said Beefer. "You're the one with the crazy bum-biting killer hamster that you told to eat me!"

"And I'll do it again, too, if you don't stand down," I said. "Only this time I'll tell him to bite off your whole hand! You'll never play Renaissance music again!"

Hammie Rex roared. Beefer flinched.

"It's over, man," I said, "I know all about your little pet."

Beefer blinked. "You do?" he said. "Then tell me what they've done with him!"

"Huh? How should I know? All I know is that wherever your quadcopter sprays that Funchos

Flavor-Wedge dust, that's where Squirrel Kong attacks!"

"Sam," said Beefer, dropping his fighting stance, "if this is one of your dumb so-called humor jokes, I don't get it."

I pointed the camera at him. "Admit it! That thing in your hand is a remote control for a quadcopter!"

"This?" said Beefer, holding it up for me to see. "This is a ham radio."

"But I know you planned Squirrel Kong's 'assault' on SmilesCorp. You wrote it down in your psycho journal!" I held up his notebook.

"You read my diary!" shrieked Beefer in a higher tone than when Hammie Rex chomped his posterior. Even through the ninja mask, I could tell he was mortified.

"What? I mean, okay, yes, I guess technically I did." I felt a little embarrassed when he put it that way.

"That's really low, Sam. Even for you," said Beefer. "Look, since you read my *private* diary, you ought to know the only reason I'm here is to get him back!"

He threw both hands out like it was obvious.

"Your penmanship was terrible," I said. "Get *who* back?"

"Michael Perkins!" said Beefer. "For a nerd, you sure are dumb, Sam."

"Wait. You think your pet snake is here? Inside SmilesCorp?"

"I know he is!" said Beefer. "Michael Perkins was my best friend . . . my only friend. But Smiles-Corp took him from me."

I'd heard that rumor, but my mom said it wasn't true. "Why do you think that?" I asked.

"Because Michael Perkins ate part of their precious invisible doughnut and they wanted to pump his stomach to get it back! It was one of a kind and they spent a zillion bucks to invent it. Or maybe they even wanted to study the effects of how it made him turn invisible or something! After Science Night, when your mean hamster flung my defenseless boa constrictor out the window, I never saw him again. I came back and searched and searched the school parking lot and I didn't find any sign of him."

"Did you ever think that maybe Michael Perkins just slithered away? Personally, I wouldn't want to live with you."

"No!" cried Beefer, his voice cracking as he spoke. "He was my best friend! Whenever he got out of his cage he always came back! Always!"

"Okay, okay," I said. I was starting to realize that Beefer felt the same way about Michael Perkins as I did about Hamstersaurus Rex. He really loved that snake.

"Anyway, I started investigating online," said Beefer. "There's this awesome one-hundred-percent-reliable website called truthblasters.com—"

"Come on," I said, shaking my head. "That website is for crazy conspiracy theories."

"No, it's not!" cried Beefer. "On Truthblasters, you can learn all about crop circles and how werewolves are real and the secret stuff that multinational corporations are secretly doing to take over the world without us even noticing!"

"Wow. Can you just listen to yourself for a second?"

"Oh, and I suppose the idea of a remote-controlled quadcopter that sprays Funchos Flavor-Wedge dust to make a giant squirrel attack specific targets sounds more realistic to you, huh, Sam?"

"Okay. Fair point," I admitted.

"Anyway," said Beefer, "I looked on Truth-blasters and I found out that SmilesCorp has this crazy lab where they secretly do weird genetic testing to create their snacks and stuff. I'm *sure* that's where they're keeping Michael Perkins."

"I don't get it," I said. "If all you care about is rescuing your snake, then why were you spying on me at the Antique Doll Museum?"

"How self-centered can you get?" said Beefer. "I wasn't spying on *you*. I was spying on SmilesCorp. With binoculars, you can see Building Seven from the ADM parking lot. And with my ham radio I can listen to the walkie-talkie conversations of the security guards. Plus I was hoping I might, you know, bump into my ex-girlfriend."

"Your ex-girlfriend?" I said, confused.

"Martha!" cried Beefer.

I had to admit, if I applied some weird Beefer Vanderkoff anti-logic to it, his explanation mostly added up. But if Beefer wasn't to blame, that meant that the real culprit behind Squirrel Kong was still at large.

"And you swear you haven't had anything to do with the twelve-foot-tall squirrel that keeps attacking Horace Hotwater Middle School?" I said.

"I swear," said Beefer. "Even though, if I'm being honest, that does sound pretty cool."

Hammie Rex growled at him.

"Look, Sam," said Beefer, "you keep blabbing about quadcopters. Well, I bet you the one you're looking for belongs to SmilesCorp. The company just started a pilot quadcopter delivery program for their online store. It was all over the news."

"Really?" I said.

Beefer nodded. "And you should read some of the weird stuff they get up to in their Genetic Research and Development Lab that doesn't ever get reported on. This is where they made the invisible doughnut that was all full of nasty fish DNA. Right here in Building Seven!"

"Beefer, my mom works at SmilesCorp. She said this is the accounting department."

"No! Don't you see? That's what they *want* us to think," said Beefer, tapping his head frantically. "If there is a giant squirrel terrorizing Maple Bluffs, I'm sure SmilesCorp had something to do with it. In fact, I guarantee you that it came out of this very building."

I was starting to feel sick. Beefer Vanderkoff was making sense. How could SmilesCorp not be behind Squirrel Kong?

"The truth is through this door," said Beefer.

Beefer pointed to the heavy steel door to Building Seven.

"Except it's locked," said Beefer, "so I'll never be able to get Michael Perkins back."

He leaned against the wall and slowly slid down until he was sitting on the ground. He was making soft squeaking noises. It took me a moment to realize that Beefer Vanderkoff was crying.

I looked at Hammie Rex. Hammie Rex looked at me. Neither one of us knew what to do.

"Uh. It's okay, man," I said. "You could get another snake."

"I don't want another snake!" said Beefer, tears

and snot now soaking his ninja mask. "He was my friend and nobody will believe me. Nobody will listen to me. Nobody will help. There's no way inside."

I knew how I would feel if Hamstersaurus Rex was sent away to the Irma Bergstrom Memorial Home for Troubled Small Pets. I would feel exactly the way Beefer did now.

I unzipped my backpack and rummaged around at the bottom until I found what I was looking for.

"You're wrong, Beefer," I said. "There is a way inside."

I swiped my mom's official SmilesCorp ID card. The red light on the lock turned green.

CHAPTER 15

"**HERE, PUT THIS** on," whispered Beefer as he pulled out a wrinkled piece of black cloth and handed it to me.

It took me a moment to realize that it was a second ninja mask.

"I always carry a spare," said Beefer. "Technically it's forbidden by the sacred Bushido code of the ninja brotherhood for you—an untrained nerd who hasn't earned his clear belt—to wear it, but you don't want them to see your face. They've got security cameras."

I couldn't believe I was teaming up with the guy who had once given me a pancake-batter swirlie. I pulled the mask down over my head and nearly gagged.

"Ugh," I said. "Beefer, it smells like . . . you."

"That's the smell of true ninja power," said Beefer. He bowed.

I tucked Hammie into my shirt pocket and the three of us stepped inside Building Seven. I immediately saw that Beefer was right about one thing: the dark room we entered didn't look like an accounting department at all. There were microscopes and test tubes and huge industrial-sized lab equipment that I couldn't possibly guess the purpose of. Building Seven was definitely a laboratory of some sort.

Beefer did an overly elaborate ninja pointing gesture at a door marked "PROTOTYPES—FOOD AND BEVERAGE DIVISION." We tiptoed through it.

This room was filled with industrial-sized stoves, ovens, and refrigerators. A large dry-erase board showed scribbled notes for a new type of sogginess-resistant jalapeño popper. We were in some sort of SmilesCorp test kitchen.

We passed a row of vacuum-sealed glass

cases, each containing a single snack food item. The first held a doughnut that was continuously shifting through all the colors of the rainbow. Perhaps it

was the next iteration of the invisible version? I admit this one was more appealing. The swirling color effect was hypnotic, but I wondered how it was achieved. Chameleon DNA?

Another nearby glass case was fogged with condensation. I wiped it away with my sleeve and saw that it held a single chocolate chip cookie that appeared to be frozen solid. Long icicles trailed off it. A digital thermometer inside the case showed the temperature was –100°C. This was odd (who freezes a perfectly good chocolate chip

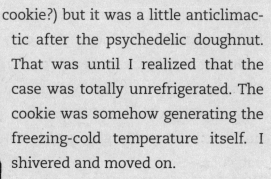

cookie?) but it was a little anticlimactic after the psychedelic doughnut. That was until I realized that the case was totally unrefrigerated. The cookie was somehow generating the freezing-cold temperature itself. I shivered and moved on.

The next case held a slice of pepperoni pizza that looked totally normal. Oddly it was plastered with stickers that read "DANGER! DO NOT TOUCH!" I stared at the case for a minute, wondering what could be so dangerous about an apparently normal-looking slice of pizza—

ZAP! I blinked as a bright bolt of electricity arced from one pepperoni to another.

"What kind of crazy snacks were SmilesCorp working on in here?" I said.

"I sure hope they do a Maple Syrup and Pickles Funchos Flavor-Wedge flavor," said Beefer, glancing around. "That's something everyone would enjoy."

"Dude, you still want to eat snacks made by the company that abducted your only friend?"

Beefer looked crestfallen. "You're right. I guess I should probably start a boycott or something. At least until I get Michael Perkins back. They better not have done anything to my beautiful bouncing baby boa—"

Just then Hammie Rex snorted. The little guy heard someone coming. I gave Beefer some frantic shushing and hiding gestures and both of us squeezed into a large cabinet that was full of tubs of ingredients with labels like "Sugar," "Flour," and "Partially Hydrogenated Frog Chromosome Extract." It was an uncomfortably tight fit. My leg was somehow folded behind my back and Beefer's elbow was poking me in the face. Out in the test kitchen I saw a bobbing flashlight.

Sure enough, a SmilesCorp security guard passed through the room, whistling to herself. After she was gone, Beefer and I waited a full minute before we felt safe enough to come out of the cabinet. Close one.

"If Michael Perkins is here, that's where they must be keeping him," I said as I pointed to another heavy door marked "ANIMAL CONTAINMENT AND MODIFICATION."

We passed through it into a long, dark hallway lined with rows of animal cages. The ones nearby contained standard white lab mice, but the hooting, scuffling, and growling of other animals filled the air. If SmilesCorp created Squirrel Kong, my gut told me that this was where it had happened.

"What's that?" said Beefer, nervously pointing to a heavy iron cage on the floor nearby. A creature crouched in the shadows of the far corner.

I pulled out my UltraLite SmartShot camera, still set to night-vision mode, and pointed it at the animal. On the display, I could see now that the cage held a lean brown rabbit-like creature.

"Don't worry. I think that's just a hare," I said. "Which is like a rabbit but—"

I saw the hare turn toward me, its eyes glowing a vivid green on the camera's display. It pulled its lips back to reveal rows of glistening, razor-sharp teeth. From my pocket Hammie Rex whined. I panned the camera down to the label at the base of the cage. It read "Specimen #3010, *Lepus arctos horribilis*— Grizzly Hare." I snapped a photo as I slowly backed away from the cage.

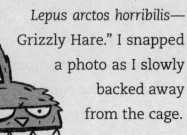

"I'm really starting to get creeped out here," said Beefer. "It's like that movie *The Mutant Beasts of Dr. Murder* but, like, actually scary."

"This place is horrible," I said, looking at the animal cages around us. "What does any of this have to do with snack foods or health supplements or quadcopter deliveries?"

"I told you, Sam," said Beefer. "SmilesCorp is up to some bad stuff."

We now passed by more rows of apparently normal white mice, except these cages all had high-tech electronic food dispensers attached to them. Each of the dispensers had a large red button on the outside.

"Huh," I said, "I wonder what the red buttons are. Obviously we can't push them because—"

Beefer punched the button on the dispenser attached to the cage. A single Funchos Flavor-Wedge tumbled out of the dispenser and down into the mouse's cage. The mouse gave a crazed squeak and flew at the salty snack.

By the time Hammie even caught the Flavor-Wedge's scent, the white mouse had finished devouring it and was licking the orange dust off its whiskers. It had the same crazed look that I'd seen so many times before.

"All these mice are totally addicted to Funchos Flavor-Wedges," I said.

"Well, they are a delicious snack," said Beefer, "and good for you."

"What? They're not good for you."

"Agree to disagree," said Beefer.

As we continued onward, the hallway split into a T. In the middle of the fork stood a massive cage, at least twenty-five feet by twenty-five feet. It held one plastic bowl the size of a small trash can of water and another one filled with acorns. The cage was empty, though. I checked the label at the bottom. It read:

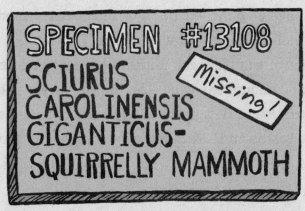

SPECIMEN #13108
SCIURUS
CAROLINENSIS
GIGANTICUS-
SQUIRRELLY MAMMOTH

Missing!

The word "Missing!" was handwritten on a sticky note.

"This is it!" I cried. "This has got to be Squirrel Kong!" I snapped a pic.

"Really? Sure looks a lot like an empty cage to me, Sam," said Beefer. "Did Squirrel Kong eat an invisible doughnut, too?"

"You're right," I said. "This is a start, but I have to find out if there's any more hard evidence about Specimen #13108 somewhere in the lab."

"And I need to find Michael Perkins so I can give him smooches!" said Beefer.

We stared at each other for a moment.

"Okay," I said, "let's split up and meet back here in ten minutes."

Beefer ninja-scuttled down the left fork of the hallway and I headed right. Eventually I came to an office. One wall was covered in portraits and the other had a computer bay with four identical computers side by side. Through a single high window I saw a patch of night sky outside. I took Hamstersaurus Rex out of my pocket and put him on the floor.

"All right, Hammie," I said. "You keep watch while I see what's on these computers."

Hammie Rex chirped in agreement and stomped off to stand guard behind me.

I tried to log in to all of the computers, but they were all password locked. Luckily, the second terminal from the left had the deeply unimaginative password "Smiles1234." I searched through the hard drive until I found a folder full of numbered files. Sure enough, there was one called 13108.txt—Squirrel Kong's specimen number.

I opened it. It was a text file that seemed to be a case history of Specimen 13108. As far as I could tell it had something to do with performing a series of extremely complicated tests on a gray squirrel. But the language of the file was way too technical for me to understand. I sighed. I was pretty sure I'd found my evidence, but I had no idea what it proved. I would need to save the file for later. Maybe with time and effort I could actually comprehend what it meant. I briefly considered emailing 13108.txt to myself but I thought better of leaving behind any internet history on the SmilesCorp computers. Instead, I popped the universal memory card out of my camera and inserted it into the computer. I saved 13108.txt to the card.

Across the room, Hammie made a plaintive noise. I turned to see the little guy staring up at the wall of portraits. He gave another soft whine.

"What's up?" I said. "What are we looking at?"

Once I got closer I saw that the portraits were all paintings of the lab chiefs of the SmilesCorp Genetic Research and Development Lab. They dated back fifty years and led all the way up to the lab's present chief, a severe-looking bald man named Gordon Renfro. Hammie stood on the floor and gazed up at the portrait hung next to Renfro's: a kindly looking elderly woman with thick glasses. She kind of reminded me of my grandma. The plaque below her portrait said she was the previous lab chief and her name was Dr. Sue Sandoval.

It also said her tenure ended last year. Hammie whined again.

I'd never seen him like this. It was odd, but I couldn't help but get the feeling that Hamstersaurus Rex somehow *knew* this woman. On impulse, I popped the memory card back into my UltraLite SmartShot and snapped a picture of the wall of portraits.

Hammie Rex whined again and hopped up and down. I picked him up and held him closer to Sue Sandoval's picture.

"What?" I said. "Is there something you want me to see?"

Hammie cooed happily and nuzzled the portrait. An instant later, I heard the noise of footsteps coming. I dashed across the room and dove under the computer bay.

"Sam!" cried Beefer. "I found Michael Perkins! But they did *something* to him!"

I crept out on all fours to see Beefer holding a boa constrictor. But after a moment I noticed that something wasn't quite right. Instead of scales, the snake's body was covered in bright green feathers. As Michael Perkins coiled around Beefer's shoulders I saw that two undersized wings now sprouted from his body. Instead of his fanged mouth, he now had a little orange bird beak.

"He's, like, part parakeet or something," sobbed Beefer. "They made my beautiful bouncing baby boa a parakeet!"

"You're right," I said, completely dumbfounded. "He's, like, a . . . boakeet now. Or maybe a feather boa?"

"Waaaaaah!" Beefer burst into tears. Michael Perkins squawked and flapped his tiny wings in dismay.

"Shhhhh. It's, uh, okay, man," I said. "Maybe we can figure out how to fix him. But first we've got to—"

I heard a faint buzzing sound from outside the window. I turned. Sure enough, the shape of the quadcopter

was silhouetted against the night sky. Hammie Rex growled.

"Oh no," I said.

Outside in the darkness, I heard the telltale shriek of Squirrel Kong.

CHAPTER 16

"**BEEFER, WE'VE GOT** to get out of here right now," I cried, running toward the hallway.

I turned to see that he wasn't following me.

"What's the use?" he said, still blubbering, as he slumped to the ground. "My best friend is a boakeet now. A boakeet! That's not even a thing. I can't be best friends with a boakeet. He's useless."

Michael Perkins squawked pitifully, reflecting Beefer's angst.

"Snap out of it, man!" I said. "He might be a little . . . different, but he's still Michael Perkins.

He's not useless. Deep down he's the same coldblooded rodent-eating constrictor you always loved. Anyway, none of that will matter if we're here when Squirrel Kong shows up. Now stop crying because that's what, uh, nerds do."

Beefer looked up at me and wiped his face with the back of his hand. "You're right, Sam," he said, standing up again. "If I sit here crying then I'd be no better than you."

"Whatever. Just come *on!*"

BOOOOOM! The wall to the lab burst inward, spraying bricks and rubble everywhere. Beefer shrieked. The hulking furry shape that stood in the hole let out a bloodcurdling cry.

Before I could stop him, Hamstersaurus Rex roared and leaped out of my pocket. He hit the ground running and charged, top speed, right at the beast. He meant to finally have his rematch with Squirrel Kong.

"Hammie, no!" I cried.

But it was too late. Hamstersaurus Rex sprang at Squirrel Kong and opened his jaws wide for an epic dino-chomp. Squirrel Kong reared back and kicked Hamstersaurus Rex in midair. The little guy sailed clear across the room—right over my head—and smacked against the wall with a light thud. Then he fell to the ground, limp, beside me. I scooped him up and stuffed him into my pocket, just as Squirrel Kong gave another enraged bellow. The quadcopter buzzed around overhead like an angry hornet crop-dusting the room with Funchos flavoring.

"Follow me!" I cried to Beefer.

Beefer blinked and then we both started to run, leaving Squirrel Kong and the copter behind us. Red lights were flashing throughout the building and a siren now wailed. A cool automated female voice spoke over the intercom. "Warning. Security breach in Building Seven: Animal Containment and Modification. Warning. Security breach in Building Seven . . ."

Beefer and I ran through the animal lab, retracing our steps. Behind us I could hear the quadcopter and Squirrel Kong smashing its way through walls, splintering furniture, upsetting cages, and crunching scientific equipment. Each bellow sounded angrier than the last. The sheer terror of the other animals in the lab had reached a fever pitch. Their barks and howls and screams were nearly as loud as the SmilesCorp alarm system. A horde of lab rats with slippery-looking fish scales ran past us on the floor. Squirrel Kong must have upset their cages.

Up ahead I saw the beams of two flashlights bobbing toward us in the dark. Security guards! I yanked Beefer aside and we hid behind a big tank full of murky water. The creature inside swam in incredibly fast circles. I didn't get a good look, but it seemed to have a yellowish reptilian body speckled with black spots. I glanced down at the label: "Specimen #5869, *Acinoyx mississippiensis*— Cheetahgator." The two guards raced past us to

confront the "security breach."

"What the heck is going on!" whispered Beefer. He looked absolutely terrified.

"Hang on!" I said. I had to check on Hamstersaurus Rex. I gently removed him from my pocket. The little guy was still limp. He wasn't moving. I held my breath and put my finger on my chest and felt for signs of life. Nothing. Then, a tiny heartbeat. He was still alive! Hamstersaurus Rex was alive! The giant squirrel kick had knocked him unconscious, though. I carefully put him back into my pocket.

"Sam, what *was* that thing back there?" said Beefer, staring into the darkness in the direction we'd come from.

"I told you," I said. "It's Squirrel Kong!"

"So there really is a giant squirrel?"

"Of course there is!"

"Wow. I totally didn't believe you before," said Beefer. "I mean, honestly, Sam, you make a lot of stuff up. You basically have what I'd call an overactive imagination—"

"Shhh!"

I saw the flashlights returning. The guards ran right past us again, heading back the way they had come at top speed. Their faces were utterly terrified. An office chair came flying down the hall after them. It smashed into a rack of animal cages, toppling them and freeing three capuchin monkeys and a dozen bullfrogs.

Beefer and I waited a moment for the guards to disappear, then we made a break for it. Together we ran through the door back into the food and beverage division, along with an ever-increasing number of terrified animals, fleeing the mayhem of Squirrel Kong. We ran past the glass cases along with otters and iguanas and armadillos that slithered and hopped and scuttled along the ground between our feet. Occasionally I'd catch an eerie glimpse of an animal that didn't look quite right: a duck that seemed to be covered in fur; a dachshund that might have had six legs; another shiny, scaled rat. Finally, Beefer and I made it out the side door where we'd entered the lab. A stream of animals followed us out, rushing past our feet and into the night. Behind me the sound of Squirrel Kong's rampage continued unabated. The very foundations of Building Seven seemed to shake, making me wonder if the entire structure might collapse. The scene was utter pandemonium.

Beefer and I ran together for a few dozen feet. Hamstersaurus Rex was still unconscious in my pocket, and Michael Perkins draped forlornly across Beefer's shoulders. I grabbed my bike and hopped on, ready to ride hard for home. We turned to go our separate ways.

"Sam, wait," said Beefer.

I paused.

"Look, I just want to say that . . . even though I'm super tough and I'm not scared of stuff . . . I maybe wouldn't have gotten Michael Perkins back without you. So, you know . . ." He trailed off, mumbling something that was too faint for me to hear.

"What?" I said.

"I said thank you!" said Beefer. "Jeez, how many times do you need to hear it?"

Gratitude from Beefer Vanderkoff! That was as strange as anything I'd seen inside SmilesCorp. Stranger still was what was about to pass my lips.

"Hey, thank you, too, Beefer," I said, "for helping me get what I need to save Hamstersaurus Rex."

Beefer nodded. "Sam, I want you to know that tonight you have demonstrated the qualities of a true ninja warrior. I'm pretty sure I don't hate you." He ninja-saluted me and then dove into the bushes.

I took off and didn't stop pedaling until I'd made it all the way home.

Hammie Rex suddenly came to as I was gently putting him back into his "Extension Cords" habitat. I was no hamster doctor, but the little guy didn't seem to be operating at 100 percent. Squirrel Kong's kick had left him groggy and tender. He was moving slowly and not putting any weight on his back left foot. I hoped none of his injuries were serious.

"You're lucky to be alive," I said, shaking my head. "I asked you before, but now I'm telling you: you can't ever fight Squirrel Kong again. You hear me? Never again."

He blinked and gave a little pained moan. I snuck back inside my house, returned my mom's ID to her purse, and climbed into bed. She was still snoring away in her bedroom, just like before. Outside, the wind rustled the leaves. And some-where, Squirrel Kong raged.

CHAPTER 17

THE NEXT MORNING, I got up early to watch the local news. I sat through the whole broadcast waiting to hear something about the disastrous night at the largest employer in Maple Bluffs. They didn't mention it. They didn't mention any animals except a bit at the end about a sheep in a neighboring county that had prevented a burglary. I checked the internet, too. Nobody had any stories about the incident. Not even the weirdos on truthblasters.com were talking about it.

I ate my breakfast cereal lost in thought. Who was behind the attacks? Why was Squirrel Kong menacing its own creators? Perhaps the answers were in the file I'd saved from the lab computer.

I opened 13108.txt again. It was just as incomprehensible, columns and columns of numbers and dates and metric system units I'd never even heard of. My eyes nearly crossed looking at it. I still wasn't smart enough to understand it. I only knew one person who was.

Out in the garage, I found Hammie in his hypoallergenic habitat. He stood up, a little unsteadily. I dropped a stack of peanut butter and jelly sandwiches in beside him.

"I'm going to leave you at home today so you can get better, dude," I said.

He started to growl in protest but then winced. Even he couldn't pretend that he was back to full health.

I hopped on the bus to school. When I got there, I stalked the halls until I caught a glimpse of Martha through the crowd.

"Martha!" I called out. "Hey, Martha!"

Martha glanced at me. Then she quickly ducked into the girls' bathroom and didn't come out again. I waited until the first bell rang and caught up to her as we made our way to class. She was conspicuously pretending to read a Portuguese phrasebook as she walked.

"Martha, I really, really, really need your help," I said. "Look, I have this data file and you're the only one who might be able to—"

"Where is the library?" she said quietly.

"Huh?" I said. "You know it's on the second floor."

"*Onde é a biblioteca*," she said to herself as she nudged past me and kept on walking.

All day long Martha successfully avoided me. Wherever I was, she wasn't. Whenever I found her she seemed to disappear.

At lunch Dylan slammed her tray down next to mine.

"So, are you pumped for Saturday?" said Dylan. "I know it's just an exhibition match and we're really doing it to increase interest in the sport. But between you and me, we are going to make the Flingmasters wish they never left West Blunkton."

"Who?" I said, distractedly staring at Martha across the cafeteria. "Also, where?"

"The First Annual Maple Bluffs Disc Golf Exhibition Tournament," said Dylan, frowning. "It's Saturday at Cannon Park. You said you're going to be there an hour early in appropriately colored face paint. You didn't forget, did you?"

"No, no, I didn't forget," I lied. "I'm just a little distracted today . . ." I told Dylan about everything that happened the night before.

When I was finished, she was incredulous. "So you teamed up with Beefer?"

"Yeah."

"Beefer *Vanderkoff*? The guy who once forced you to eat your own knit cap?"

"Uh-huh. I think he might have even technically made me a ninja."

"And his pet snake got turned into . . . a bird?"

"Well, it was like half a bird. Imagine a half bird, half snake."

"I can't really imagine that," said Dylan. "Look, Sam, obviously I believe you and everything." She paused.

"But," I said, crossing my arms.

"*But* wouldn't everyone have heard about it if

SmilesCorp had gotten destroyed by a twelve-foot-tall squirrel beast?"

"SmilesCorp didn't get destroyed, just the secret animal lab and the weird food-testing facility that they claim is their accounting department! Look, I'm telling you, something very bad is going on at SmilesCorp. Something downright evil."

"But your mom works there," said Dylan. "They employ half the town. They're sponsoring our disc golf tournament. Their CEO, Nils Winroth, is even throwing out the first disc. They can't be *all* bad, right?"

"Dylan, SmilesCorp is putting fur on ducks!" I said, loud enough that several kids nearby turned to stare at me. "Fur. On. Ducks!"

"Sam, please don't take this the wrong way, but I think you've been under a lot of stress recently," said Dylan. "Maybe you should just take it easy for a little while."

"You *don't* believe me, do you?" I said. "You say you do but you don't!"

"Of course I do!" said Dylan. "I'm trying to be a good friend, it's just—"

"You want proof, then look at these pictures!" I pulled my UltraLite SmartShot out of my backpack and began to scroll through the photos I'd taken inside Building Seven. I couldn't believe it. One after another, they were dark and blurry, impossible to make out.

"I'm not sure what I'm looking at," said Dylan. "Are these pictures of the inside of your mouth?"

"No, that's a fearsome Grizzly Hare!"

"Oh." Dylan turned the camera sideways. "Okay. Yeah. I guess I see it?"

I could tell she didn't. "Well, I obviously should've used the flash," I said. Finally I came to the only photo that was clear: the wall of SmilesCorp lab chief portraits. "Here, look at this. These are the people who run this creepy facility!"

"Huh, that old lady looks kind of sweet," said Dylan, looking at Dr. Sue Sandoval.

"Whatever," I said, popping the memory card out of my camera. "The pictures don't matter. I have a data file saved on this card that scientifically proves Squirrel Kong is real."

"Well, that's great news," said Dylan. "What does it say?"

"How should I know? The one person I know who can *possibly* decipher it won't even talk to me!"

I was practically yelling now. The cafeteria had fallen quiet all around us. It seemed that all of Horace Hotwater Middle School was staring at me. Everyone except Martha Cherie, that is. She was rapidly folding and unfolding a rice paper crane.

"Hey, um, I know that lunch is a time for maxing and/or relaxing," said Mr. Duderotti, sidling up to our table. "But would it be uncool if I told you you were being a smidge loud?"

"No, Todd," said Dylan. "That wouldn't be uncool. We understand. We'll keep it down."

"What's on that memory card, anyway?" said Mr. Duderotti.

"What?" I said. "Nothing." I stuffed it in my pocket.

"Hey, wait a minute. Todd's a scientist," said Dylan. "Maybe he could interpret the data for you—"

"No," I said.

"Data?" said Mr. Duderotti. "I *love* me some data. Interpreting data gets me mad stoked. What's the data, homeslice?"

"Nothing. I'm done eating." I picked up my tray and quickly left.

For the rest of the day, I bided my time. Martha might be able to avoid me at school, but there was one place she did have to talk to me. After the final bell rang, I hopped on the crosstown bus to the Antique Doll Museum.

"Yes, I'd like the full deluxe doll tour, to learn about all the different weird dolls you have here," I said to Martha, now clad in her Antique Doll Museum blazer and pin.

"Well, I'm sure we can find you a fully trained docent," said Martha, scowling. "I'm just an intern."

"No, I talked to Patricia in the admissions booth and she assured me that you know more about the creepy dolls than anyone who is actually paid money to work here," I said, crossing my arms.

"Fine," said Martha. "If you want me to show you the dolls then I'll show you the dolls. And I'll answer questions about dolls and only dolls. Nothing else."

"Fine," I said. "That's what I came here for: all these scraggly old dolls. Like that one."

Martha mechanically gestured to a small, shriveled figure displayed on a nearby shelf. "This doll dates all the way back to 1892 and happens to be made entirely of beef jerky. She's on permanent loan to the Antique Doll Museum from the Greater Tucson Institute for Jerky Art. Her name is Misty."

"Cool," I said. "And is it okay if I take Misty and put her in my pocket and walk right out that door?" I pointed to the museum exit.

"What?" said Martha. "No. Obviously, that would be stealing."

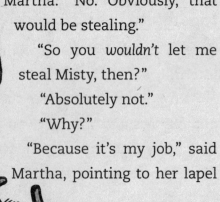

"So you *wouldn't* let me steal Misty, then?"

"Absolutely not."

"Why?"

"Because it's my job," said Martha, pointing to her lapel

pin. "In case you forgot our conversation from forty-two seconds ago and/or how to read: I'm an Antique Doll Museum intern."

"Interesting," I said. "So if you *didn't* work here, then it would be okay for me to steal Misty."

"Again, no," said Martha, frustrated. "Stealing is wrong, Sam. Even you should be able to understand that."

"Wow," I said, stroking my chin, "it's almost like a person has a duty to do what's right, even when it's *not* their job."

Martha frowned and crossed her arms. She sighed. "All right, fine," she said at last. "I'll look at the data file."

"Yes!" I said. "Thank you, Martha! You're saving Hamstersaurus Rex! And, look, I'm so sorry about lying before. I should have never let you resign as Hamster Monitor."

Martha nodded. "Well, at least you're taking the job seriously. There's no other reason you'd visit the Antique Doll Museum twice in a week."

"I mean, I think these old dolls are pretty exciting, too," I said. "It's cool that you're into them."

"Come on, Sam," said Martha. "You have to stop with the mendacity."

"Okay, you're right," I said, looking around the museum at the hundreds of pairs of shiny glass eyes staring back at me. "I'd feel more comfortable in an abandoned hospital haunted by the ghosts of dead clowns."

Martha escorted me to the back offices of the Antique Doll Museum. They were just as deserted as the rest of the place. It was early evening and it seemed that the minimal staff had mostly gone home for the day. We walked through a dusty glass door that said "Technology Center" into a room full of old green filing cabinets and piles of loose papers. Martha fired up an ancient-looking computer and popped my memory card in.

". . . Are these photos some sort of abstract art

project, Sam?" said Martha, scrolling through my pictures of the lab. "Like are you trying to make some sort of statement about the fundamental nature of blurriness and the lack of proper lighting?"

"Forget those, just look at 13108.txt!"

Martha opened the file and began to read it. Her face turned serious.

"How did you get this file?" she asked. "No, wait, don't tell me. I don't want to know."

I shifted in my seat impatiently. "So, um, what do all these numbers mean?"

"Hang on. Let me finish," said Martha. "Wow . . . Fascinating . . . Huh. Very interesting . . ."

"What? What's interesting and what's fascinating? What?"

"Well, it appears to be the case history of Specimen #13108."

"Right, that's Squirrel Kong."

"Apparently, SmilesCorp scientists gave a genetically modified squirrel a concentrated dose of something called Huginex-G."

"Whoa, that's crazy! Is it crazy? What's Huginex-G?"

"Looks like it's a proprietary compound that SmilesCorp developed to make Halloween pumpkins bigger. Anyway, by giving Huginex-G to Specimen #13108, they were able to *temporarily* increase the squirrel to colossal size for up to one hour."

"Temporarily? So somebody is still dosing the squirrel with more of that Huginex stuff?"

"According to their logs, they were never able to make #13108's size change permanent. I guess they needed to add more receptors to her genetic code or something?"

"You lost me at the end there, but wait . . . Squirrel Kong's a girl?"

Martha squinted at me. "And why *wouldn't* Squirrel Kong be a girl?"

"I mean, I don't know, I just never thought—I mean, Squirrel Kong just doesn't *seem*—I mean . . . I don't know!"

"Women can do *anything* that men can do, Sam! Even be rampaging, bloodthirsty rodent monster beasts!"

"Okay, point taken," I said.

"Hmm, it looks like they deliberately induced

a Pavlovian aggression response in Specimen #13108 to a particular flavoring."

"I'm guessing Funchos Flavor-Wedges."

Martha nodded.

"But why?" I said.

"Doesn't say here," said Martha, with a shrug. "But Squirrel Kong was apparently so dangerous that, for safety's sake, SmilesCorp developed an antidote to the Huginex-G that they called 'Microcyll.' It's administered via nasal spray."

"Nasal spray!" I said. "That must be what Mr. Duderotti used when he spritzed Squirrel Kong in the face and she shrank down to normal size. But how did he get his hands on . . ." I suddenly had a nagging feeling in my gut. "Martha, can you please open the last photo that I took?"

"Sure," said Martha.

She clicked on the thumbnail picture of the SmilesCorp lab chiefs, and now it displayed full size. Sue Sandoval's twinkly eyes stared back at me through her glasses. But I wasn't interested in her.

"Zoom in on that portrait to the right, the bald guy."

Martha did. Now the frame was filled by the sharp-featured face of SmilesCorp's current Lab Chief: Gordon Renfro.

"Does that man look familiar to you?"

"Uh, no," said Martha. "I mean, he looks a little like my old Portuguese tutor. But Flávio moved back to Funchal."

"Imagine if Gordon Renfro, here, had sunglasses?" I said. "And a ponytail?"

Martha used the rudimentary drawing tools in the image program to color in two black circles over Gordon Renfro's eyes and add a long, squiggly ponytail on his head. She gasped.

"SmilesCorp has a plant working inside Horace Hotwater Middle School," I said. "Gordon Renfro? More like Todd Duderotti!"

Just then we heard a noise behind us. On the other side of the glass door, the silhouette of a figure quickly ducked out of sight. Martha and I stared at each other, our eyes wide. Someone had been listening to everything we had said.

CHAPTER 18

MARTHA AND I stood and crept toward the door. Whoever was listening had frozen on the other side of the glass, just out of sight.

"Who's there?" I asked.

No response. I turned the handle and pushed. With a slow creak, the door swung open.

"Norton, is that you?" asked Martha. "Are you on a routine patrol?"

No response. I stepped out into the dimly lit hallway. It appeared to be empty. Just then I heard something behind me. I turned to see a stack of boxes marked "Ginny Gossamer—Gift Shop Replica." The pointy tip of a brown leather shoe poked out from behind the stack. Someone was crouching there, in the darkness.

I turned to Martha. She shrugged, her eyes as big as saucers.

"Gotcha!" I cried, leaping toward the boxes.

"Hey, I know you! Sam Gibbs, winner of the Little Mister or Miss Muscles competition," said Roberta Fast, standing up from her hiding place. She grabbed my hand and shook with just the right amount of firmness.

"Ms. Fast, were you, um, listening in on our conversation?" said Martha.

"No, I was just counting these boxes!" said Roberta Fast. "Let's see. One, two . . . seven. There are seven boxes. Yep, everything checks out."

"Are you sure you didn't hear anything?" I asked. "Anything that might have sounded weird?"

Roberta Fast bit her lip. "Okay, I admit it. I overheard everything! SmilesCorp putting spies in our public schools and creating mutant killer animals that they've unleashed on an unsuspecting public! It's juicy stuff. Evil, of course, but juicy."

"Well, it's all true," I said.

"Sam, I worked at that company for nine years," said Roberta Fast. "I believe you."

"Thanks," I said. "It's good to finally hear that from someone and know they mean it."

Roberta Fast shook her head. "Honestly, this is *exactly* why I left. SmilesCorp has no ethical center! Profits above all. They're capable of anything."

"But if it's all true, why wasn't the latest Squirrel Kong attack on the news?" asked Martha.

"I'd bet SmilesCorp didn't even report the attack to the police. They'd rather keep something like that internal than reveal that they've created a deadly monster squirrel in their labs that's now menacing our town."

"Ms. Fast, you're a public relations director," said Martha. "You have contacts in the media. Maybe you could use them to expose SmilesCorp's negligence and irresponsible behavior. According to Sam, Squirrel Kong is just the tip of the iceberg. They're putting fur on ducks and such. I don't know if that's technically illegal, but it certainly sounds wrong!"

"Hmm," said Roberta Fast. "We'd need an

event. Something really big and splashy to get people's attention."

Martha blinked. "The First Annual Maple Bluffs Disc Golf Exhibition Tournament! The event is sponsored by SmilesCorp and the CEO is going to be there this Saturday!"

"Nils Winroth is making a public appearance in Maple Bluffs in two days?" said Roberta Fast, her eyes widening.

Martha nodded.

"Then that's perfect," said Roberta Fast. "We'll get in front of the cameras and ambush him with a bunch of questions about killer squirrels. Then we'll hit him with the incriminating information contained in that file. We'll force Mr. Winroth to explain everything, live on tape."

"Hang on. Does it have to happen *at* the tournament?" I said.

"You never know where Nils Winroth is going to be," said Roberta Fast. "This might be the best shot we get for months. Maybe years."

"But aren't we maybe losing focus on the real culprit?" I said. "Nils Winroth isn't the one controlling Squirrel Kong. Unless he attacked his own company."

"Maybe he did," said Roberta Fast, shaking her head ominously. "I wouldn't put it past him. That man is totally unscrupulous. And anyway, the *ultimate* responsibility for Squirrel Kong does lie with SmilesCorp, doesn't it?"

She was right. Still, I didn't relish the thought of disrupting the tournament that Dylan had put so much effort into planning.

"Can't we just go to the police instead?" I said.

"Sure, we could *try* going to the cops first," said Roberta Fast, "but I doubt they would believe you. Or understand your data file, for that matter. And even if they did, building a case against SmilesCorp might take years. Do you really want a twelve-foot-tall killer squirrel to be on the loose, rampaging around Maple Bluffs, for years?"

"Someone might get seriously hurt," said Martha.

"Trust me," said Roberta Fast. "If we make Squirrel Kong—great name, by the way—a national news story, that's what will get the attention of the police. That's what will bring the real culprit to justice."

"I don't know," I said.

"Sam, as much as I hate not immediately going to the proper authorities in every situation," said Martha, "this does seem like it might be more effective."

"Okay, okay," I said. "As long as we can prove that Squirrel Kong is real, and clear Hammie Rex's name, I guess we should do it. So what do you need from me?"

"The data file, for starters," said Roberta. "I need to reformat it and print it out as digestible info-graphics and camera-ready pie charts, so you can wave them around in Nils Winroth's smug face."

"Wait, *I'm* going to be the one confronting him?" I said.

"It will be you and Martha," said Roberta Fast. "Our messaging is going to be much more effective coming from two cute kids and not a former employee of the company who resigned on moral grounds. Besides, Sam, you're the one with the personal connection to this Squirrel Kong story."

"It's okay, Sam," said Martha, "I can do most of the talking. I've studied many of history's greatest orators."

"Fine," I said, and I handed Roberta Fast the storage disc.

"Leave the rest to me," said Roberta Fast. "I'll go whip up a press release and get some hard-hitting squirrel gotcha questions ready. Let's meet at Cannon Park half an hour before the event to coordinate."

I still felt unsure. "And you're positive there isn't any other way?"

"Sam, you're the one who faced this deadly mutant squirrel beast," said Roberta. "If you think it's best not to confront SmilesCorp at this event, then we don't have to do this. Say the word and I'll call it off."

I took a deep breath. "No, I guess this is our best shot."

"All right, then, kids, I'll see you both Saturday. It feels great to use my PR skills for good!" She grinned and shook Martha's hand and mine again. Then she disappeared into her office.

Martha and I took the crosstown bus back through town, together.

"I hope the plan works," I said. "But I still wish I knew who was flying the Funchos quadcopter."

"I'm stumped," said Martha. "But you know there's at least one person who's still not telling the truth."

"Gordon Renfro," I said.

At home I found Hamstersaurus Rex asleep in his hypoallergenic box. He blinked when I woke him up to feed him a plastic container of my mom's leftover beef stroganoff with some marshmallows on top. The little guy only ate about half of it.

"What's wrong with your appetite? Are you still sore?"

He gurgled weakly. I was worried about the little guy. Squirrel Kong's kick must have really packed a wallop.

The next morning, I left Hamstersaurus Rex at home again to recuperate and rode the bus to school. When I got there, I made a beeline to Room 117. I was surprised to see that it had been fully repaired, and then some. All the equipment was state of the art. Now everything was bright white or gleaming steel. It had the slick, futuristic look of a SmilesCorp laboratory.

"Good morning, Mr. Duderotti," I said.

"What up, Sam!" said Mr. Duderotti, extending his fist.

I left him hanging. "Or maybe I should call you by your real name."

"Todd?" he said.

"How about Gordon?" I said.

He flinched, but a millisecond later, he was all smiles again.

"Okay, rad," said Mr. Duderotti, closing the door to the lab. "And while we're goofing and riffing like a pair of cutups, I'll call you Gordon, too. Yep, we're just a couple of Gordons, having a dope chill sesh. Say, Other Gordon, what're your thoughts on hoverboards? Because I'm literally obsessed—"

"You can cut the act," I said. "I know you took a job at our school under an assumed identity. I know your real name is Gordon Renfro."

"Say whaaaaat?" said Mr. Duderotti. "That

accusation is, like, totally bananagrams."

"I don't know why SmilesCorp put you here, but I do know it has something to do with Squirrel Kong. Sorry, I mean Specimen #13108."

Mr. Duderotti paused for a long time. His phony grin twisted into a scowl. "Listen, little homie, I *don't* work for SmilesCorp," he said, his voice now strangely different. "But if somebody did, I bet they'd just be trying to get their company's gnarly intellectual property back."

"So you admit that SmilesCorp scientifically created a giant squirrel?"

Now he grimaced. "Exqueeze me? No idea what you're talking about, broseph. If you're referring to the band Giant Squirrel, I told you I like their first album but everything after that was pretty corporate." He crossed his arms and shrugged. "I'm curious where you got such a wack idea that you obviously have no credible proof for."

"No proof? You don't think a photo of your portrait hanging inside a secret genetic testing lab is proof?"

I'd clearly caught him off guard. His eyes

flashed with anger and he stepped toward me, causing me to involuntarily back up toward a shelf of chemical containers.

"If you had proof like that, it would be totes surprising," said Mr. Duderotti, pulling his sunglasses off. "Because it would totes mean that you'd totes illegally trespassed on SmilesCorp property. Epic fail. Can you imagine being linked to a recent break-in at a major international corporation?"

"What?" I said. "I don't know what you're, uh, talking about."

"Oh snap, and it would be even worse for you if you'd taken something, like, say, a data file from one of the computers. That would be an extremely serious crime, the consequences of which would pretty much be the opposite of rad." Mr. Duderotti scratched his jaw and pretended to think. "Come to think of it, doesn't your mother work at SmilesCorp, Sam?"

This time it was me who was taken aback. "What? Yeah, she does," I said. My voice sounded weak. "That doesn't have anything to do with—"

"Hmm. You know, it'd be a *total bummer* to *the*

max if all your snooping somehow *affected your mother's job*," said Mr. Duderotti.

I was at a loss for words. I moved my mouth but nothing came out.

"What's the matter?" said Mr. Duderotti. "Did I kill the vibe by dropping a major truth bomb, amigo?"

Something on the shelf behind me caught my eye. It was a row of aerosol canisters that looked somehow familiar. Their labels read "Microcyll"— they were bottles of the Squirrel Kong antidote spray that Mr. Duderotti had used before!

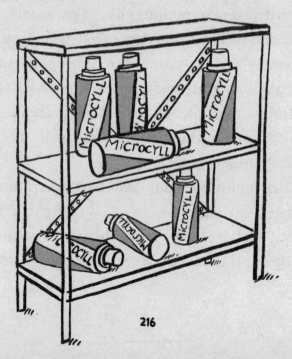

"You just tell SmilesCorp to leave my mom out of it, okay," I said.

"Hey, man, I don't work for SmilesCorp," said Mr. Duderotti. He put his sunglasses back on, popped his collar up, and grinned.

"If you don't work for them, then explain that!" I pointed over his shoulder.

He turned and chuckled. "That's a diagram of a plant cell," he said. "You're grasping at straws, homie."

"Whatever," I said. "But if I've got a photo of your lab chief portrait, you might want to stop and consider what else I took photos of inside that Animal Containment and Modification lab of yours."

At this Mr. Duderotti's jaw fell open. It was obvious that he was terrified of SmilesCorp's secret experiments—cheetahgators, grizzly hares, furry ducks—becoming public knowledge.

"You know, I think we're done here," I said as I walked past him out the door. "Great chill sesh, Todd."

As I walked down the hallway, I replayed the conversation in my head. Mr. Duderotti was a

SmilesCorp spy, perhaps up to his own nefarious schemes, but I honestly felt like he wanted to capture Squirrel Kong as much as I did. Maybe more. He wasn't the one flying the quadcopter. I only hoped he wouldn't notice that I'd swiped a canister of his Microcyll spray. At least the next time I encountered Specimen #13108, I'd be prepared.

CHAPTER 19

AT LUNCH, I caught Dylan up to speed.

"Mr. Duderotti is a SmilesCorp plant!" I said under my breath. I was worried that he might be "chilling" somewhere nearby.

"Who, Todd?" said Dylan, cocking her head in disbelief. "No way, Sam. I don't believe it. Todd is just a cool rebel who's maybe a little misunderstood because he refuses to play by society's rules."

"Dylan, seriously, I have proof. Remember that photo I took, the one of all the paintings? Well, one of them is Mr. Duderotti!"

"I don't remember any of them being him," said Dylan.

"That's because in the portrait, he didn't have his 'cool' ponytail and 'cool' sunglasses."

"You make a good point; his sunglasses are pretty cool. Fine. Let me see that photo again."

"I can't. I don't have the picture anymore. I mean, I gave it to Roberta Fast."

"Who?"

"Remember the invisible doughnut lady?"

"Sort of," said Dylan.

"She's the new PR director of the Antique Doll Museum," said Martha Cherie, putting her tray down beside ours.

"Oh. Hi," said Dylan. Her voice sounded cold.

"Hello, friends," said Martha.

"Martha, I'm confused," said Dylan. "I thought you hated Sam's guts."

"I did," said Martha. "But he apologized and convinced me to help him by asking if he could steal a doll made of beef jerky."

"Huh?" said Dylan.

"It made sense in context," I said.

"Anyway," said Martha, "with Ms. Fast's help, we're planning to confront SmilesCorp's CEO at the First Annual Maple Bluffs Disc Golf Exhibition Tournament."

"Hang on. You're going to do *what?*" said Dylan.

"We're going to confront Nils Winroth," I said. "I found proof positive that Squirrel Kong is real. Taking that public is how I can clear Hamstersaurus Rex's name."

"You can't ambush our guest of honor!" said Dylan. "This event is incredibly important, Sam. I've been planning it for so long. It's for the good of the sport!"

"Sorry, Dylan," said Martha, "but our plan is for the good of all humankind."

"Sam, tell me this isn't happening?" said Dylan. "Tell me you didn't sign off on this!"

"Well, you know, it . . . seemed like maybe the best way?" I said, and stared at my sneakers.

"You can't be serious!" said Dylan. "You know how much this tournament means to me. You want to ruin it by turning it into some sort of publicity stunt?"

"Well, it's just that Roberta Fast knows about public relations and, uh, she thought this was the only opportunity we'd get."

"Look, Sam, I know you care about Hamster-saurus Rex. I do, too," said Dylan. "But I'm also your friend!"

"It's just that Squirrel Kong—"

"Squirrel Kong, Squirrel Kong, Squirrel Kong. All I ever hear you talk about these days is Squirrel Kong!" said Dylan, furious now. "You know, it's very odd how you're the only one who's ever actually seen Squirrel Kong."

I felt my own anger starting to rise. "Other people have seen her! Todd—Gordon, whatever you call him! He saw her!"

"That's not his story," said Dylan, crossing her arms. "Martha, have you ever seen Squirrel Kong?"

Martha hesitated. "Well, no. Not exactly."

"Thought so," said Dylan.

"Beefer saw her!" I cried.

"Right. Beefer Vanderkoff," said Dylan, "a super-reliable witness."

"You know, *you* might have seen her, too," I said, "if you hadn't made up some lame excuse not to come with me to the SmilesCorp lab!"

"Guys, maybe keep your voices down," said Martha, glancing around the cafeteria.

"I didn't make up a lame excuse!" said Dylan. "That lame excuse was real. Sam, I've helped you every chance I got. I wasted a whole week looking around the woods behind school for Squirrel Kong. Now you can't hold off for one single day, to not screw up the most important day of my life?"

"But time is of the essence," I said. "Squirrel Kong's a real threat to public safety!"

"Squirrel Kong's not a real threat," said Dylan, "because Squirrel Kong is not real!"

A silence fell over the cafeteria as her words rang in my ears. I knew I was about to say something I might regret.

"You know what's not real?" I cried. "Disc golf!"

Dylan stared at me in shocked disbelief. Then she picked up her tray and stormed off.

"Wow, Sam," said Martha, "you should probably be a little more careful about what you say. Might I suggest studying some of history's greatest orators?"

The rest of the day passed less eventfully. A few kids tried to follow me home but I was used to it now. I doubled back and shook them off my tail. At dinner, I ate my tuna pasta, lost in thought.

I woke up early the next morning. I showered and dressed. Then I poured myself a bowl of cereal and turned on the Weather Channel. It was going to be a gray, windy day. I had two hours until the First Annual Maple Bluffs Disc Golf Exhibition Tournament. I could still contact Roberta Fast and tell her to call the whole thing off.

"Wow, you're up early for a Saturday, aren't you Bunnybutt?" said my mom, yawning.

"Mom, can I ask you a question?"

"Sure."

"Did you hear anything about a giant squirrel attack on SmilesCorp, Building Seven?"

"A giant squirrel attack on the accounting department? No. They closed that building for fumigation. Is that what you're talking about?"

I sighed. "Can I ask you another question? Should a person do the right thing, even if it might hurt the people they care about?"

"Well, that's a very complicated question," said my mom. "I guess it would depend on if you're sure it's the right thing and how badly it would hurt them."

"What if I'm not sure of either of those things?"

"Hmm. Then I guess you've got to just trust your conscience."

"I was afraid you'd say that," I said with a sigh. "Look, Mom, SmilesCorp is up to some bad stuff. They created Squirrel Kong and now she could hurt somebody. We're planning to prove Squirrel Kong is real by telling everyone what they've done. Even though it might cost you your job. . . . I hope you can forgive me."

My mom gave a wry smile. I could tell she still wasn't taking me seriously. "Well, if you think that's the right thing to do, Sam. But I'm curious, how are you going to 'tell everyone'?"

"Well, I'm working with Roberta Fast to confront the CEO when he—"

"Wait. Who did you say you're working with?" said my mom, her face now stricken with fear.

"Roberta Fast," I said. "You remember, she used

to work with you at SmilesCorp but now she's the PR director of the Antique Doll Museum."

My mom grabbed me tight by both shoulders. "Of course I remember Roberta Fast. Sam, I don't want you anywhere near that woman."

"What? Why?"

"She's crazy. After she got fired for the invisible doughnut debacle at Science Night, she vowed to get revenge on the entire company. It was an awful scene. She had to be escorted off the premises by the police."

"Hang on," I said. "She got fired? I thought she resigned, you know, for ethical reasons."

My mom shook her head gravely. "No, Sam, as they were dragging her out she swore she'd get back at 'all those responsible for destroying her life.' I never told you this because I didn't want to scare you but . . .

she even mentioned that hamster at your school. Can you imagine how deranged you'd have to be to blame a sixth-grade class pet for losing you your job?"

My blood ran cold. "That is . . . scary," I said.

"Scary is an understatement," said my mom. "Sam, you have to stay away from Roberta Fast! I have no idea what she's capable of."

"I think I do," I said. It had suddenly become clear to me who might want to get back at Horace Hotwater Middle School, SmilesCorp, and Hamstersaurus Rex.

CHAPTER 20

"MARTHA, COME ON . . .** come on . . . answer." I listened to the phone ring three, four, five times. "Answer!"

Then I heard a voice on the other end: "*Olá, quem é?*"

My heart sank. "Oh, I must have the wrong number." I started to hang up.

"Wait, Sam? Is that you?" said Martha. "Sorry, I'm expecting a call from my *new* Portuguese tutor, Faustino. What's up?"

I told her everything my mom just told me.

". . . and I'm worried Roberta Fast is the one controlling Squirrel Kong!" I said. "She's flying the quadcopter!"

"Wow," said Martha. "She's been *such* a good PR director for the museum, I never would have guessed she's an evil mastermind."

"Well, she is. And I think it's up to us to stop her. Do you have *any* idea where she could be right now?"

"I don't," said Martha, "But . . ." She trailed off.

"But what?"

"Well, the Antique Doll Museum might have her address on file somewhere?"

"Can you call and ask them for it?"

There was a long pause. "Sam, I don't think they're going to be authorized to give out personal information like that. It's against the rules."

"So we have to break the rules," I said. I could practically hear her flinching on the other end of the phone. Seconds of silence passed. "Martha, are you still alive?"

"Uh-huh," she said. "I just need to do a little deep breathing. Yes, Sam, I think you're right. We might have to *break the rules*."

"Okay," I said. "Meet me at the Antique Doll

Museum in forty-five minutes."

I hung up the phone and ran out to the garage to get my bike. I opened the lid to Hammie's "Extension Cords" habitat. The little guy was on his feet, almost like he was waiting for me. He looked healthy now and I could see the old fighting spirit gleaming in his eye. I couldn't help but smile. I reached into the cage and took him out.

"Gotta go," I said. "I need to find Roberta Fast, quick. In case something bad happens, I just want you to know, I love you."

I gave him a kiss on top of his head. He gave a little love burp and nuzzled my face.

"Hey! I knew it! Sam's keeping Hamstersaurus Rex at his house!" cried a voice.

I turned to see the faces of Caroline Moody and Jimmy Choi crowded together, staring through the garage window. I sighed.

"Sam, that hamster's a criminal!" cried Jimmy. "Open this garage door right now!"

"Sorry, I'm afraid I can't do that, Jimmy," I said. I scooped Hammie Rex up and dropped him into my shirt pocket. The little guy would have to go with me now.

"If you surrender peacefully, things will be easier for you when I call Animal Control," cried Caroline.

"If I surrender peacefully, Squirrel Kong will strike again and Roberta Fast might get away with it," I said.

I shrugged and picked up my bike and carried it back into my house.

"Bunnybutt, do you still need a ride to Dylan's tournament?" said my mom, confused.

"No, Mom. Change of plans."

"Why are you carrying your bike into the—ACHOOOOOOOOO!" She interrupted herself with a deafening hamster-induced sneeze that rattled the windowpanes.

"I can't go out in the garage," I said, handing her a tissue. "Too much heat."

Just then our doorbell rang.

"Don't answer that," I said as I made my way to the back door. The bell rang again.

"Wow, being twelve seems like a nonstop thrill

ride," said my mom. Then she gave another one of her explosive sneezes. "Yuck. I must be coming down with something."

I snuck out into our backyard. Then as quickly and as quietly as I could, I dragged my bike through several adjoining yards and into Mr. Greco's boxwoods. I poked my head out. The street ahead was all clear.

Suddenly, Caroline and Jimmy jumped out from behind the Wilkersons' seasonal fall display of scarecrows playing touch football.

"End of the line, Sam!" said Caroline, standing across my path.

"Guys, I'm in a hurry," I said. "Can you turn me in to the authorities tomorrow? I promise you I'll still live in the same house then."

"Nope," said Jimmy. "You're going to sit tight while I call the Department of Animal Control right now. And keep the hamster where I can see him."

Hammie snarled. Jimmy pulled out a cell phone and started to dial. I had to think fast.

"I'm just curious, Jimmy, why are *you* the one calling to claim the three hundred dollars? Didn't Caroline spot me first?"

"We'll split the reward," said Jimmy, holding the phone to his ear.

"Huh? We didn't discuss that," said Caroline.

"Caroline, we both saw him at the same time," said Jimmy.

I could hear the phone ringing.

"Um. No we didn't," said Caroline. "Sam said I spotted him."

"Also—and I don't mean to complicate things—but *technically* I think the check has to have one person's name on it," I said. "So I don't really think you two can split it, per se."

"We can't?" said Caroline.

"One of you would have to cash it and then

give the other half the money," I said. "You two trust each other, right?"

Jimmy and Caroline paused for a moment.

"Look, I'm just going to make this call," said Jimmy.

"No, you're not!" Caroline snatched the phone out of his hands.

"Hey, give me that back!" cried Jimmy.

"Hello?" said a confused Animal Control operator on the other end.

"You're not going to steal my reward!" cried Caroline, holding the phone out of his reach.

They were still arguing back and forth like that when I took off, pedaling as fast as I could toward the Antique Doll Museum.

When I got there, I found Martha outside, looking grave. She seemed like she was rehearsing what she might say to a judge. I locked my normal bicycle beside her strange tandem one.

"Sam, is what

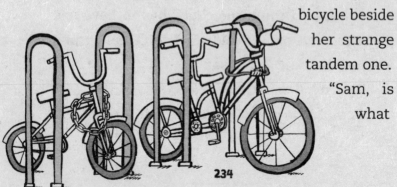

we're about to do going to put me on a path that leads to a life of crime?" whispered Martha. "Like the one you seem to be headed for?"

"We're doing the right thing," I said.

Hammie poked his head out and gave a growl of support from my pocket.

Martha gasped. "Hamstersaurus Rex has been with you the whole time?"

"Yep," I said. "Aiding or abetting a fugitive hamster. Just another line on my rap sheet."

As we walked past the counter, Martha greeted Patricia, the ticket taker.

"Greetings, Patricia! I'm just here to volunteer, as per normal," said Martha, in a strange high-pitched voice. "Like I usually do."

"Fine. Don't care," said Patricia. She didn't look up from her book.

"But my great-grandfather Étienne, on his deathbed, bestowed upon me his lucky pocket watch," said Martha. "It's silver and emblazoned with the head of an elk. Such a noble beast! Anyway, my whole life I've always cherished this timepiece for personal—"

"Get to the point!" said Patricia.

"Martha forgot something in Roberta Fast's office," I said. "Can you let us in?"

"Knock yourself out," said Patricia. She took a key off her key ring and tossed it to me. Then she returned to her book.

"Whew! That was a close one!" whispered Martha.

I shook my head.

We entered the museum and made our way to the back office. At the end of the hallway was a door that said "Roberta Fast" in block letters on it. A small Do Not Disturb sign hung on the handle.

I unlocked the door to the office and we ducked inside. The room was dark and filthy. Every surface was covered in clutter or trash, and the place reeked of Funchos Flavor-Wedges. On a filing cabinet in the corner was an empty cage. A board on the wall had dozens of newspaper clippings pinned to it: stories about SmilesCorp's quadcopter delivery program, events at Horace Hotwater Middle School, Principal Truitt being honored by the Lions Club, and more. They all had strange handwritten notes scrawled on them. From my pocket Hammie Rex gave a soft continuous growl.

"Martha, I think this is actually where she was planning it all," I said as I looked around the office. The hairs on the back of my neck were standing on end.

"Yeah," said Martha, glancing nervously over her shoulder. "It feels like she just left."

As I took a step, I accidentally kicked a spent Funchos Flavor-Wedge canister and sent it spinning across the ground. I looked down to see that there were dozens more just like it littering the floor.

"Well, that explains the smell," I said.

"Hey, check this out," said Martha, holding up a thick binder. "'Flight Manual for SmilesCorp 4B-800 Delivery Copter. Not for Distribution. Internal Use Only.' She must have somehow stolen the quadcopter from SmilesCorp and taught herself to fly it."

"Yep. Just like she stole these," I said. Inside the top drawer of her desk were several bottles labeled "Huginex-G." They were all empty, except one. "I think she's nearly down to the end of her supply."

I picked up the nonempty bottle and shoved it in my backpack.

"What?" cried Martha. "Sam, you can't disturb a crime scene! Haven't you ever watched TV?"

"I know, but I can't risk leaving it here," I said. "Without any more Huginex-G, Squirrel Kong will turn back into a normal squirrel."

Martha nodded. "Here's what's starting to worry me," she said. "The squirrel cage is empty. Where do you think Roberta Fast is right now?"

"This might give us a clue," I said. Taped to the far wall was a giant map of Maple Bluffs with various locations hand-marked: Horace Hotwater Middle School, SmilesCorp, and others I didn't recognize. A building on Front Street was labeled "TERRIBLE DRY CLEANER WILL DESTROY!!!" Another house said "HODGE'S HOUSE. LAUGHED AT ME IN THE 9th GRADE. REVENGE WILL BE MINE!!!"

"These are all her Squirrel Kong targets," said Martha.

"Yep. And I'm thinking she's exactly where she said she would be." I pointed to the map. On it, Roberta Fast had repeatedly circled Cannon Park, site of the First Annual Maple Bluffs Disc Golf Exhibition Tournament. Beside it, four words were written in a spidery scrawl: "NILS WINROTH WILL PAY!!!"

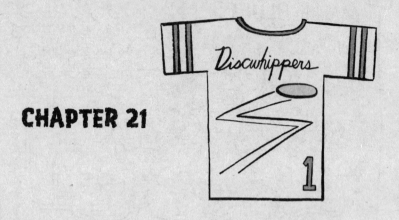

CHAPTER 21

"**T**HE TOURNAMENT IS starting in twenty minutes!" cried Martha. "How are we going to make it in time?

"No idea," I said. "But I need to make a quick phone call first."

"Meet you outside!" said Martha as she dashed out the door and I started to dial.

A minute later, I joined her on the sidewalk in front of the Antique Doll Museum. Martha looked dejected.

"Sam," she said, "I've done the math, and if we ride our bikes, there's no way we're going to make it to Cannon Park before Nils Winroth makes his opening remarks."

"What about the bus?"

"I already checked the schedule. There's not one coming for another fifteen minutes."

"Wait," I said. "Your bike has two sets of pedals. What if—"

"Yes!" cried Martha, doing the calculations in her head. "Operating at peak efficiency, we should be able to go roughly twelve percent faster on my tandem! We'll *just* make it."

Martha and I scrambled onto her bike and we both pedaled as hard as we could through the town of Maple Bluffs. Soon the tree line of Cannon Park loomed ahead. Powerful gusts of wind tore at the branches.

We rode on the park's bike path toward the tournament site. Soon we saw a fifty-foot-tall temporary digital scoreboard looming above the trees. It was emblazoned with the SmilesCorp smile logo. Rows of bleachers had been set up on the green beside it. The tournament was surprisingly well attended. The stands were mostly full and at least three local news stations had sent crews to cover the event. I had to hand it to Dylan, it really had generated interest in the sport.

As Martha and I approached, the sounds of the national anthem floated toward us. The three Discwhippers—Dylan, Dwight, and Tina—stood in a line, singing along, their maroon and mauve jerseys flapping in the wind. Coach Weekes stood proudly beside them. As the song crescendoed, I saw him brush back a patriotic tear. Nearby, in plain purple T-shirts, were what must have been the West Blunkton Flingmasters and their jowly red-faced coach. Principal Truitt stood between both teams, her hand on her heart. And there was Mr. Duderotti off to the sidelines, mouthing the words and bopping slightly to the beat. Behind them all, a twisting course of chain-and-wire disc golf goals stretched out into the distance.

"We made it in time!" I cried, between gasps for air.

"Tandem bicycle!" cried Martha, pumping her fist.

"There! That must be him," I said, pointing to a trim, well-dressed blond man in wire-rim glasses, with two beefy security officers flanking him on either side.

As the anthem ended, Principal Truitt took the mic. "Welcome, one and all, to the First Annual Maple Bluffs Disc Golf Exhibition Tournament! This event would not have been possible without the generosity of SmilesCorp. And the man I'm about to introduce helped put our little town on the map with his visionary decision to relocate the headquarters of a major international corporation right here to Maple Bluffs. Please welcome the global CEO of SmilesCorp, Mr. Nils Winroth!"

The audience applauded as Nils Winroth stepped up to the podium.

"Good morning, Maple Bluffs," said Nils Winroth in a slight Swedish accent. Then he paused for a long time. ". . . Creativity is about making connections. The human being is the only animal that laughs. We alone ask ourselves the big questions: What is gravity? Where do clouds come from? How can a brightly colored plastic disc be made to soar like an eagle into one of those barrel thingies? Today we celebrate connections and creativity and laughter. Today we celebrate humanity."

The crowd erupted in thunderous applause.

"So inspiring," said Martha, lost in the moment and clapping along with the rest.

Above the noise I heard a familiar sound. I scanned the sky. Sure enough, there was a tiny speck approaching fast.

"You know," said Nils Winroth, "when I was a small boy growing up on my father's dill farm north of Malmö, I always—"

"Everyone, you have to leave!" I cried, leaping in front of the podium. "It's not safe here!"

The entire crowd stared at me.

Nils Winroth scowled ever so slightly. "Hem. Who is this fellow?"

"Ha-ha. Don't mind him!" cried Coach Weekes, trying to block me from view. "Very unenlightened kid! Long way to go on his spiritual journey!"

Principal Truitt ground her teeth, both fists balled. "Sam Gibbs, you are being extremely insulting and inconsiderate of Nils Winroth's valuable time. Sit down. Now!"

"I'm not trying to be rude—"

"Don't listen to him," said Dylan, yelling over me. "No need to answer his questions. Let's get things going. How about that coin toss to see who throws first?"

"Dylan, please! I'm trying to *warn* everyone," I said. "About that!"

I pointed to the quadcopter. It was close now, hovering about a hundred feet over the bleachers. The whole crowd turned to look up at it. Heavy wind buffeted it from side to side.

Nils Winroth laughed. "Ah, this is all you're worried about? Don't be afraid, young man. That's just one of our new SmilesCorp delivery copters." He grinned and waved at the copter and beckoned it closer.

"No, Mr. Winroth!" I cried. "Don't let it get near you. The woman flying it wants to hurt you!"

"I'm afraid you are very much mistaken," said Nils Winroth. "Soon, it will be quite common to see such copters flitting to and fro, delivering books and toothbrushes and pet-grooming devices, and other—"

"Stop right there, Sam!" cried Caroline Moody as she ran across the green. Jimmy Choi was running right beside her, huffing and puffing.

"How many small children are going to interrupt me, today, I wonder?" said Nils Winroth, frowning.

"Sam Gibbs has Hamstersaurus Rex in his pocket!" yelled Jimmy Choi and Julie Bailey in unison.

The crowd of mostly Horace Hotwater middle schoolers and parents gasped.

"Let the record show that Julie and I *simultaneously* reported this information," cried Jimmy Choi, "and thus believe that it's entirely reasonable for us to receive two separate three-hundred-dollar checks in our own names!"

"Mr. Gibbs, is this true?" cried Principal Truitt. "Do you have the rogue hamster that nearly destroyed our school with you, at this very moment?"

The copter was hovering lower now, barely ten feet off the ground. It was wobbling toward Nils Winroth in the wind.

"Yes, I do," I said, "but that's not what's important!"

"It wasn't Hamstersaurus Rex that did the attacks, Principal Truitt. He's not the dangerous one," cried Martha. "You can trust me because I don't have a history of fabricating fanciful stories, like Sam."

"Mr. Winroth, please," I cried, "for your own sake, don't let that quadcopter get near you!"

"No need to have fear, young ones," said Nils Winroth, reaching out to it, "this little flying copter is the future of—"

PFFFFF! The copter fired a pressurized Funchos blast. But a last-second gust of wind knocked it off course. Instead of hitting Nils Winroth, the brightly colored flavoring cloud hit the person standing beside him.

"Blech! What's going on?" cried Coach Weekes, wiping the sticky dust from his eyes. "Why am I seeing orange?" He'd been thoroughly coated from head to toe.

"What the heck?" said Dylan, her jaw falling open.

"Um," said Nils Winroth, looking mystified. "Quadcopter is not supposed to do this. Perhaps a malfunction?"

His bodyguards shrugged.

"Why is all I taste Tangy Honey Habanero?" wailed Coach Weekes. "Am I dead?"

Before I could get to it, the quadcopter darted vertically away out of reach.

With an earsplitting roar, Hamstersaurus Rex

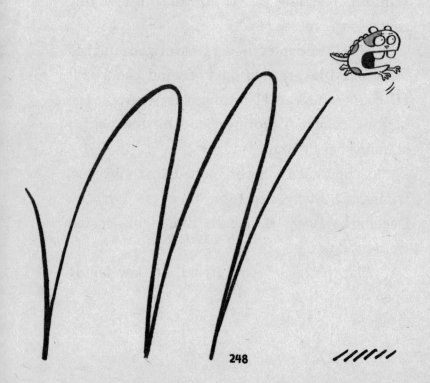

burst out of my pocket and landed on the ground. The smell of all the Funchos Flavor-Wedge dust sent him over the edge. He was about to frenzy.

"Hammie, no!" I cried.

"Everyone remain calm," said Principal Truitt in a terrified voice into the mic. "Please don't panic at the sight of this deranged hamster! Any sudden movements might incite Hamstersaurus Rex to kill!"

CHAPTER 22

"WHY'S THE HAMSTER** looking at me like that, Gibbs?" asked Coach Weekes. He took a nervous step backward. "He looks . . . hungry."

"Hammie, please!" I cried. "Calm down. Take a deep breath."

Hamstersaurus Rex gave a vicious snarl and took a step toward Coach Weekes.

"Don't eat me!" squealed Coach Weekes.

"What is happening?" said Nils Winroth. "Everyone is afraid of a hamster? I don't understand."

"Come on, Hammie," I said in a steady voice.

"You're the rock in the middle of the sea! A rock doesn't go psycho over Funchos dust. Remember?"

Hammie took another step toward Coach Weekes. From the corner of my eye I saw that Mr. Duderotti was moving toward him with his hands outstretched. Hammie took another step.

"Don't just do what everyone expects you to do! You're better than that! You are the rock, so be the rock! *Just be the rock!*"

Hammie paused.

"Be the rock!"

Hammie blinked.

"Be the rock!"

The little guy shook himself like he was covered in water.

"Be. The. Rock."

Slowly, Hammie turned to stare back at me, a little dazed. I could see that the crazy look in his eyes was gone. He grinned. An instant later, he came bounding back to me, trailing slobber the whole way.

"You did it!" I cried. "You conquered your addiction to junk food!"

The little guy leaped into my outstretched arms and I hugged him close to my chest.

"You know, Hamstersaurus Rex doesn't look very dangerous," said Omar Powell.

"He looks cute," said Tina Gomez.

"I assure you, that animal is a cold-blooded engine of destruction!" yelled Principal Truitt into the mic. "He totaled my car! My car was nice!"

The little guy rolled over onto his back and I started to rub his belly. His dino feet began to kick in the air. The crowd gave a spontaneous "Aaaaaaw."

"Wow," said Wilbur Weber, "what a delightful ending. I can't believe everything worked out so—"

"Oh my God, what is that thing?!" shrieked Julie Bailey from the bleachers.

As one, the crowd turned in the direction she was pointing. A massive furry shape stomped out of the trees and onto the disc golf course. In the cold light of day I could see a crazed, remorseless

look in Squirrel Kong's coal-black eyes.

There was a moment of stunned silence, as the crowd realized they were looking at a real-life monster. Then, they panicked. Screaming attendees of the First Annual Maple Bluffs Disc Golf Exhibition Tournament fled in every direction. Omar Powell dove under a trash can. Julie Bailey made a beeline for the woods, shrieking the whole way. Mr. and Mr. D'Amato herded their three boys behind them for protection. All around me, it was utter chaos. One of the news teams' cameramen threw his camera down and started to run. Hamstersaurus Rex roared again.

"Sam, the copter!" cried Martha over the din. "It's coming back!"

"Where?" I cried.

I turned around to see the copter shooting right toward me at top speed. I started to run and made it four steps before my foot caught on the tangle of microphone cables that led to the podium. For an instant I was airborne. Then I hit the ground hard, knocking the wind out of my lungs. I rolled over onto my back. The copter hovered directly above me.

PFFFFF! Dylan yanked me out of the way just in time to dodge another pressurized Funchos blast. The grass where I just had been was stained neon orange.

Hamstersaurus Rex jumped for the copter, but it had already darted up and away vertically into the sky. I heard the sound of his jaws snapping closed as he missed it by a few inches.

"Sam, I think now is when I say I'm sorry I didn't believe you about Squirrel Kong," said Dylan, helping me to my feet.

"Sorry I disrupted your big day," I said. "And sorry I said disc golf wasn't real. It's real."

Nils Winroth's two security guards rushed toward Squirrel Kong as she waded through the terrified crowd. With a mighty bellow, she sent one flying with a swift kick. The other turned and fled as fast as he could.

"Sam, I think it's time I did one of the things I do best," cried Martha. "Alert the proper authorities. Maybe Animal Control will have something that can defeat a deranged twelve-foot-tall squirrel."

"Good thinking," I said.

Martha turned and disappeared into the panicked throngs of people.

"So what the heck do we do in the meantime?" said Dylan as she watched Squirrel Kong rampaging through the crowd.

"She'll attack whatever the copter sprays."

"So we stop the copter," said Dylan.

We turned to see that it was now hovering about thirty feet off the ground, preparing for another dive-bomber-style attack.

"Allow me," said Dylan. She squinted like an Old West gunslinger. Then, from behind her back, she whipped one of her tournament-grade golf discs right at the copter. It flew with laser-like accuracy, but at the last second, a gust of wind knocked it off course, and it missed the quadcopter.

"Not fair!" cried Dylan.

Squirrel Kong bellowed with rage again.

"Out of the way!" cried Mr. Duderotti (or Gordon Renfro, if you prefer) as he shoved past me toward the oncoming beast. He had a spray bottle of Microcyll in hand.

"All right, Specimen #13108," he cried, "it's time to finally shut this experiment down!" He held his arm out heroically and spritzed. Nothing happened. Another gust must have blown the Microcyll mist in the wrong direction. Squirrel Kong blinked.

KABLAM! She casually swatted Mr. Duderotti out of the way, sending him tumbling end over end like a rag doll. Shattered pieces of the spray bottle landed on the grass, right beside his sunglasses and ponytail. He came to rest ten feet away, in an unconscious heap.

"Whoa. Squirrel Kong knocked his hair off!" cried Dylan in disbelief.

"It wasn't real hair," I said.

Just then, the quadcopter swooped again and crop-dusted the crowd with Funchos dust. Dylan slung two more golf discs at it but both were blown off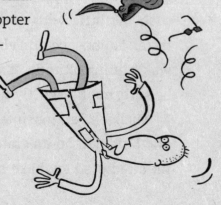

course, just like the first. The copter zipped away into the sky again.

"Ugh, it's the stupid wind!" said Dylan. "Sorry, Sam. I'm good, but I'm not *that* good."

"There's no way to get the quadcopter," I cried. "We'd have to be able to—"

"Fly, my friend!" cried a familiar voice from behind me.

Dylan and I turned to see Beefer Vanderkoff, standing on a park bench, with Michael Perkins in feathery coils around his shoulders. He spun once, twice.

"Fly like . . . something that . . . flies!" he cried as he heaved Michael Perkins into the air. At first, the boakeet looked like it was going to hit the ground like so many feet of wet garden hose. But then his little wings started to flap, faster and faster. I almost couldn't believe it. Michael Perkins was gaining altitude. It was awkward looking, to be sure, but he was flying.

Michael Perkins intercepted the quadcopter and bit down on its grabbing claw. The quadcopter attempted to shake him free, but the boakeet managed to wrap himself around the craft. The copter struggled to stay aloft as Michael Perkins continued to constrict. Copter and boakeet hit the ground together. Then, with a loud, metallic pop, Michael Perkins crushed the SmilesCorp 4B-800 Delivery Copter.

"Feather boa!" cried Beefer, striking a triumphant anteater style karate pose.

"Beefer!" I cried. "Thanks for coming."

"Well, Sam, when you called and told me that you're scared and a baby," said Beefer as he scooped up Michael Perkins, "I knew I had a duty to save you from SmilesCorp and their giant devil squirrel."

"That's not exactly how I put it, but okay, cool," I said.

"Dude, your pet snake looks weird," said Dylan.

"Not my fault!" said Beefer.

Suddenly, the fearful screams crescendoed as the panic of the crowd seemed to reach a fever pitch. Squirrel Kong scanned the area and her eyes settled on something. She pulled her furry lips back in a snarl.

I reached into my backpack and pulled out my last, best hope: the spray bottle of Microcyll I'd stolen from the science lab. Squirrel Kong plowed her way through the crowd.

"Sam, you saw what happened to Tod—Gordon Renfro," said Dylan. "The wind is too strong for that little spritzer. If you're not right up in Squirrel Kong's face, it won't work. You're liable to get killed!"

"I know!" I said.

The crowd parted as Squirrel Kong lumbered toward what appeared to be a bright orange ball on the ground. It took me a moment to realize that it was Coach Weekes, curled into the fetal position.

"Is it . . . over?" said Coach Weekes hopefully. "Has my positive mental thinking affected this situation at all?"

Squirrel Kong opened wide, picked up Coach Weekes, and put him in her mouth. She looked around. Her eyes settled on the towering Smiles-Corp temporary scoreboard. Still carrying a blubbering Coach Weekes, she lumbered toward it and started to climb.

CHAPTER 23

SQUIRREL KONG HUNG on the top of the scoreboard, with a Funchos-stained Coach Weekes now clutched in her paw. The crowd had stopped their mad panic now. They were dead silent. All eyes were on the monster and her victim, whom she periodically slurped for Funchos flavoring.

"Help me!" wailed Coach Weekes, between squirrel licks. "It was never supposed to end this way!"

"Seriously, what is wrong with this town?" cried one of the West Blunkton Flingmasters.

"Sam, we have to save him!" cried Dylan. "If

Squirrel Kong doesn't eat him, he could fall and die!"

"I know, I know," I said, "but there's no way for me to get close enough to use the antidote now."

Hammie Rex snarled on the ground at my feet. He angrily stomped around, pawing at the grass and whipping his tail back and forth.

"No, Hammie!" I said. "Beefer, is there any way Michael Perkins can fly up there and—"

"Nuh-uh," said Beefer, now clutching the boakeet protectively to his chest. "I mean, Michael Perkins isn't scared or anything, he's just tired, okay!"

Hammie growled in the direction of Squirrel Kong and spat on the ground.

"Dylan," I said, "could you nail Squirrel Kong with a golf disc from this distance?"

"Maybe," said Dylan, "but I'm not sure what that would accomplish. They're made of plastic, Sam."

Hamstersaurus Rex bit down on my pant leg and pulled it in the direction of the scoreboard.

"Hammie," I said, "I don't know how many times I have to tell you: there's no way you can *possibly* fight a twelve-foot-tall . . ."

Just then, it hit me. I rummaged around in my

backpack, where I'd stowed all the evidence from Roberta Fast's office. At last I found it: the one Huginex-G bottle that wasn't empty. I opened the lid. A bottom covering of viscous blue liquid sloshed around inside. I took a deep breath.

"All right, little guy," I said to Hammie. "This might be your chance to finally take Squirrel Kong down. Literally."

Hammie pulled his lips back to expose his fangs. He was smiling.

"Here goes nothing," I said. And I upended the Huginex-G into his open mouth. Hammie slurped down the blue syrup until there was none left.

He burped. I waited. Nothing happened. It didn't work.

"Well," I said, "I guess it was worth a—"

Then Hamstersaurus Rex started to grow . . . and grow . . . and GROW! Before my very eyes, the little guy swelled and expanded until he was huge, massive, colossal! He was nearly as large as Squirrel Kong now. Hammie opened his mouth and let out a roar that rang out through the park. Many in the crowd backed away from the now dinosaur-sized dino-hamster.

"All right, boy," I said. "Go save Coach Weekes."

Hammie Rex bounded toward the scoreboard, shaking the earth with each step. Then he started to climb. I had the impulse to film this, but then I remembered my UltraLite SmartShot once again didn't have a memory card. Stupid Roberta Fast!

As Hammie Rex got closer to the top, Squirrel Kong pulled her back foot up and kicked him, causing Coach Weekes to sway precariously in her grip. Hammie took two more jackhammer stomps to the face before he opened his mouth and chomped down hard on her paw. Squirrel Kong gave a thunderous bellow of pain.

"Aaaaaagh!" shrieked Coach Weekes as Squirrel Kong let him fall.

The crowd gasped as Coach Weekes dropped ten feet before Hamstersaurus Rex managed to catch him with his dinosaur tail.

Unfortunately, Squirrel Kong landed on Hammie's head a second later, feet first. Her

power drop dislodged his grip on the scoreboard. As he fell, Hammie somehow twisted and spun, using his tail to flick Coach Weekes, upward, past Squirrel Kong. As Weekes sailed vertically, one of his flailing arms caught hold of the scoreboard's smile-shaped SmilesCorp logo, where he clung for dear life.

Meanwhile, the two giant rodents scrabbled at each other as they plummeted the fifty feet toward the earth. Squirrel Kong was on top, forcing Hammie onto the bottom. The whole thing seemed to happen in slow motion.

"This is awesome," muttered Beefer to himself.

"She's going to crush him!" I said.

Dylan covered her eyes.

There was a deafening boom as they smashed into the ground together, blasting an instant crater in the Cannon Park green, and sending shock waves out through the soil.

As the dust settled, Squirrel Kong stood atop Hammie's motionless body.

"No!" I cried.

Squirrel Kong let out a long bellow of triumph. At the sound, most of the assembled crowd lost their calm once more. They turned and fled in terror.

"I'm not scared, I'm tired, too!" cried Beefer as he ran off with the rest.

But suddenly, Squirrel Kong went flying as Hammie kicked her off him. She skidded across the green on her back, tearing up the turf and taking out two disc golf goals and a maple sapling. Hamstersaurus Rex wasn't beaten. Not yet.

"Man, this is *way* better than the sheep that prevented that burglary!" I heard one of the local news cameramen say, as he held his ground while others around him ran screaming.

Now Hammie was on his feet and charging toward Squirrel Kong at top speed. She pawed the dirt and began to run at him. The two titanic rodents were barreling toward each other like two furry guided missiles.

They slammed together with bone-shattering force. Now they were a blur of grappling, kicking, biting, and scratching. Again, Squirrel Kong somehow maneuvered herself on top of Hammie. She managed to get a foot, then two, onto his neck and pin him to the ground. She was crushing his face into the dirt, while his stubby front paws waved uselessly. Hammy squealed in pain, but the noise was cut short as Squirrel Kong increased the pressure on his windpipe.

"He can't breathe," I said, and I started to run toward the two of them. "She's killing him!"

"Sam, wait, it's too dangerous!" cried Dylan, following me.

We were close to them now. I pulled out the Microcyll spray bottle and started toward Squirrel Kong. Hammie wheezed pitifully on the ground.

"No, Sam!" cried Dylan. "Don't do it!"

"I don't care!" I cried. "I have to try to save him!"

I was five feet away, now; almost close enough to spritz her with the Microcyll. Just a little closer . . .

From out of nowhere came a lightning-fast flick of Squirrel Kong's massive tail. I felt a flash of pain as it caught me right across the face. I had the strange sensation of the earth tumbling end over end. Then everything went black.

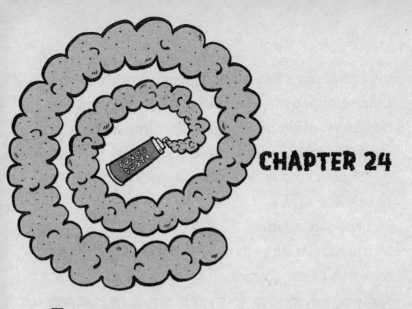

CHAPTER 24

I OPENED MY EYES to see Dylan standing over me. She was saying something but my ears were ringing and I couldn't understand what it was. My head hurt.

". . . alive?" said Dylan.

I tried to nod. She took my hand and helped me to my feet.

". . . think . . . have an idea," she said, as the ringing faded and my hearing slowly returned.

Nearby, Squirrel Kong was still crushing Hammie's neck with her feet. His eyes were open but they looked glassy. He wasn't breathing. He looked like he might not be alive at all. I shook my throbbing head and staggered toward them. Dylan stopped me. Then she showed me what she had in her other hand. It was the canister of Funchos Flavor-Wedge dust from the copter.

"Squirrel Kong will always go for the dust, right?" she said.

I nodded again.

Then Dylan ripped the seal off the canister and tossed it like a grenade. It spun through the air, spraying orange dust in a spiral cloud, and landed a few feet away from Squirrel Kong. The canister lay in the grass, pumping out the remainder of its pressurized contents. Squirrel Kong blinked and started to salivate. She was torn: Finish Hammie off or give in to her craving? At last, she abandoned Hammie Rex and went for it.

Squirrel Kong hunched over the canister, greedily slurping at the pressurized flavoring as fast as it pumped out into the air. I could see the wind wildly blowing the bright orange cloud this way and that. I crept toward her, the Microcyll bottle at the ready. She focused intensely on the flavor canister, which was starting to lose pressure. I only had a few seconds left, but I was close now . . . ten feet . . . five feet . . . two feet. Suddenly her ears twitched. She turned and stared right at me. With a shriek of pure rage she opened her jaws wide and—

BAM! Hammie Rex landed on Squirrel Kong's back, pinning her to the ground. I shoved the Microcyll bottle toward her nose and sprayed. She sniffed; then snorted; then sneezed with such force that it actually bucked Hammie off.

Squirrel Kong stood, with a wild, terrified look in her eyes, and started to run. But each step was shorter than the last. Shrinking as she went, she made it twenty feet before she was the size of a normal squirrel.

"Get her!" I cried to Dylan.

Both of us ran after Squirrel Kong as she darted across the green. We followed her down into a ditch and back out again and through a row of bushes toward the Cannon Park parking lot. There, in a far corner, sat a silver hatchback. Inside the car a woman was fiddling with huge remote control, complicated enough for a quadcopter.

"It's Roberta Fast!" I cried.

Roberta Fast turned and saw Dylan and me running toward her. Her eyes widened with panic. She reached across and cracked the passenger-side window. Squirrel Kong scrambled up the side of the car and squeezed inside.

"Stop right there!" I cried. "Don't move!"

Roberta Fast didn't listen. She started the car and peeled out, speeding past us.

"No!" cried Dylan. "She's getting away!"

Her car sped toward the exit of the lot. Roberta Fast was seconds away from escaping forever when—

CRASH! A gigantic Hamstersaurus Rex landed on the hood of the hatchback, crushing it into

the pavement and popping both of the front tires off their axle. Hammie stared through the windshield, his dino-fangs bared, and roared as loud as he could. In response, Roberta Fast screamed at the top of her lungs.

I heard sirens approaching. I got to the car and quickly spritzed Hammie Rex with a dose of Microcyll. He sniffled and sneezed and started to shrink. By the time a beige cruiser—with a strange medallion of an angry possum emblazoned on its door—pulled into the lot, he was regular old Hammie size again.

Animal Control agents Gould and McKay leaped out of the vehicle holding nets, followed by Martha Cherie.

"That's her, officers," said Martha, pointing to Roberta Fast. "She's the one."

Roberta Fast jumped out of her car and started to run.

"Stop right there!" cried Agent Gould, and she swung her net down over Roberta Fast's head and shoulders. Roberta Fast lurched to a halt. She slowly put her hands up under the net.

"Roberta Fast, you're under arrest for unlawful possession of a dangerous animal, reckless endangerment, and destruction of property," said Agent McKay as he slapped a pair of handcuffs on her.

"You can probably add a few more crimes to that list if you check her office at the Antique Doll Museum," I said.

"No!" cried Roberta Fast. "I'm not the villain here. It's SmilesCorp! SmilesCorp is evil! This is just bad optics. I'm the good guy! That's why I tried to destroy that middle school—"

"Ms. Fast, you probably don't want to say any more without a lawyer," said Agent Gould as she slammed the door, locking Roberta Fast into the back of the cruiser. Gould turned to us. "Are you kids all right?"

"Well, I'd say the First Annual Maple Bluffs Disc Golf Exhibition Tournament is a bust," said Dylan.

"And the museum is probably going to have a hard time finding a new PR director after this," said Martha.

"I think I got a tooth knocked out," I said, poking my tongue through a hole where my upper premolar used to be. "But yeah, I guess we're pretty much okay."

In a pair of heavy gardening gloves, McKay gingerly hoisted Squirrel Kong out of the driver's side of the car by her tail. She looked so puny and scared I almost pitied her. McKay carefully placed her into a cage and locked it.

"Don't worry, kids," said McKay. "She won't be getting out of here anytime soon. This here is the PETCATRAZ Pro™. Strongest small rodent cage on the—"

"We know!" said Dylan, Martha, and I in unison.

Gould cocked her head. "Say, you children haven't seen any other dangerous exotic animals around, have you?"

Dylan, Martha, and I looked at one another and shrugged. Thankfully, inside my shirt pocket, Hammie Rex didn't make a sound.

CHAPTER 25

PRINCIPAL TRUITT'S MOUTH was moving and there were definitely sounds coming out of it. If I had to guess, I'd bet those sounds were words; probably even sentences. But I wasn't listening. Instead, I was doodling in my notebook. "Mutant Half Hamster, Half Dinosaur Battling Vampire Army" was really starting to take shape.

Dylan nudged me with her elbow. "Sam, people can see you," she whispered.

She was right. Dylan, Martha, and I sat on the stage in front of the entire student body of Horace Hotwater Middle School, while Principal

Truitt spoke at the podium. I put my notebook away.

"Indeed, many of us are still trying to wrap our heads around the strange and frightening events of the last few weeks," continued Principal Truitt. "But one thing is certain: Hamstersaurus Rex displayed a courage and resolve that is rare among humans, much less small rodents. In fact, our very own Coach Leslie Weekes owes his life to his hamster heroism!"

"That gets a huge 'Namaste' from me!" cried Coach Weekes from the audience.

"Which is why I am proud to officially declare this Horace Hotwater Middle School's first Hamstersaurus Rex Day!" said Principal Truitt. "And if Hammie Rex ever returns, I will be honored to award him this."

From behind the podium she pulled out a large novelty check for three hundred dollars, made out to Hamstersaurus Rex. In the "Memo" section was written "For Defeating Giant Evil Squirrel."

The crowd applauded even though it's probably

not legal for a hamster to cash a personal check. Jimmy Choi and Caroline Moody clapped along with everyone else.

"Now," said Principal Truitt, "I'd like to introduce a student who displayed at least as much bravery as Hammie Rex. Please give a big Horace Hotwater Horace Hot-welcome to Sam Gibbs!"

"Thanks," I said, taking the microphone, "I'm not, um, great at public speaking or whatever. But if Hammie Rex was here, I know what he'd say." I leaned closer to the mic and burped.

The crowd erupted with applause.

"Wherever you are, Hamstersaurus Rex, I love you, little buddy," I said. "Also, there were two people who really helped me and Hammie a lot. And even though he's gone, so it's more of an honorary thing now, I'd like to officially award Dylan D'Amato and Martha Cherie the title of 'Hamster Monitor, First Class.'"

Dylan and Martha stood and I handed them lanyards and cage keys. Dylan grinned while Martha choked back tears.

"Thanks, guys," I said, shaking their hands.

"Oh yeah, and everybody remember to attend the rescheduled First Annual Maple Bluffs Disc Golf tournament this Saturday. It's going to be awesome!"

"Thank you, Sam," said Principal Truitt, retaking the podium. "Now I'd like to ask everyone to please return to their classrooms and, of course, have a Happy Hamstersaurus Rex Day!"

A projector behind her played my raw footage of *Chinchillazilla vs. MechaChinchillazilla* with upbeat, inspirational music over it, as students stood and started to file out of the auditorium.

"Wow, your movie's not bad, Sam," said Dylan as we walked back to class. "I liked the part when Chinchillazilla ate the Biblioteca Nacional de la República Argentina."

"Eh, I feel like the giant monsters battling each other thing has been done before." I said. "Anyway, I'm working on the script for *Final Payback: The Revenge* now. The part of Vanessa McSteel is yours if you want it."

Dylan grinned.

"Sam, I've been thinking," said Martha as she

caught up to us. "What if your new movie also had this super-smart lab tech character who was a master of foreign languages *and* disguise?"

"Well, I might have to change the story a little bit," I said. "But maybe it could work?"

"Speaking of stories," said Dylan "I still can't believe there wasn't a single one in the news about what *really* happened."

"Well, there was that one two-hundred-word online article that described it as 'a freak bear/alligator/puma attack,'" said Martha. "That almost counts."

"The worst part is they said it happened at an 'ultimate Frisbee match,'" said Dylan shaking her head. "Who plays ultimate Frisbee?"

"In a weird way, Roberta Fast was right. SmilesCorp has a lot of power in this town. Enough to keep the truth from getting out," I said. "Anyway, Beefer promised me he'd keep an eye on Building Seven. If their creepy animal lab ever reopens, he'll be the first to know."

"I still can't believe Beefer's a good guy," said Dylan.

"It takes some getting used to," I said. "Anyway, I've got something to take care of. I'll catch up to you guys later."

I split off from them and made my way toward the stairs.

The halls were mostly empty now. After making sure nobody was watching, I ducked into Room 223b. If anyone was still searching for Hamstersaurus Rex, I figured that school would be the last place they would look.

I pulled four peanut butter and jelly sandwiches out of my backpack. "All right, dude, time for your mid-morning snack. Now remember, you've got to make these last until lunchtime, so don't—"

But Hamstersaurus Rex was nowhere to be seen. He was actually gone.

The bell rang as I stepped back out of Meeting Club headquarters. Where *was* the little guy? I walked through the empty halls, looking for any sign of him, when I noticed that the door to Room 117 was slightly ajar. I stepped inside.

The lights of the science lab were off. Principal

Truitt hadn't found a long-term substitute since Mr. Duderotti-Renfro had gone on extended "medical leave."

From the back of the room I heard a little growl. I opened Mr. Duderotti's desk to see Hammie Rex, gnawing on a balsa wood model of a pterodactyl skeleton.

"Come on, Hammie," I said as I hoisted him out of the drawer. "You have to be more careful."

He gurgled and licked my face and I couldn't help but laugh. I extended my index finger to give him the world's tiniest high five. Then I tried to slide the desk drawer shut, but something stopped it from closing. I tried again, but it seemed to be bumping up against some obstruction. I fumbled around underneath the drawer and pulled out a manila envelope that had apparently been taped to the underside but had come loose.

"INTERNAL USE ONLY" was stenciled across it in bold letters. I unwound the string tying it closed. Inside the envelope were two folders. The first was labeled "SC Specimen #13108." It was filled with pages and pages of surveillance photos and information, SmilesCorp's dossier on Squirrel Kong.

The second folder was labeled "SC Specimen #00001." I opened it and gasped. On the first page was a photograph of Hamstersaurus Rex. Beside it was a sticky note that read "Neutralize and Recover."

TOM O'DONNELL is the author of *Space Rocks* and its sequel, *For the Love of Gelo!* He has written for *The New Yorker*, *McSweeney's*, and the show *TripTank* on Comedy Central. His comic strips have been featured in *The New York Press* and *The Village Voice*. He lives with his family in Brooklyn, New York.

TIM MILLER is a satirical illustrator who specializes in picture books. He illustrated *Snappsy the Alligator (Did Not Ask to Be in This Book)* by Julie Falatko, which *Kirkus Reviews* praised in a starred review as a book "with bite." Tim studied at the School of Visual Arts, where he earned his BFA in Cartooning. He lives in Queens, in New York City.